Three Dreams

By

Roberta M. Alleman

This book is a work of fiction. Places, events, and situations in this story are purely fictional. Any resemblance to actual persons, living or dead, is coincidental.

© 2002 by Roberta M. Alleman. All rights reserved.

No part of this book may be reproduced, stored in a retrieval system, or transmitted by any means, electronic, mechanical, photocopying, recording, or otherwise, without written permission from the author.

ISBN: 1-4033-8606-4 (e-book)
ISBN: 1-4033-8607-2 (Paperback)

Library of Congress Control Number: 2002095185

This book is printed on acid free paper.

Printed in the United States of America
Bloomington, IN

1stBooks - rev. 01/02/03

DEDICATION

This book is dedicated to my parents,
Marlene, Joyce and Ron.
I thank them for their help and belief in me.

Table of Contents

DEDICATION	iii
PREFACE	vii
11:26 p.m. June 1	1
7:45 a.m. June 2	8
9:04 a.m. June 02	14
1:30 p.m. June 2	28
9:10 a.m. June 3	33
4:50 p.m. June 3	35
1.30 p.m. June 4	39
7:28 p.m. June 4	44
9:27 p.m. June 4	46
11:49 p.m. June 5	50
6:30 a.m. June 5	55
11: 20 a.m. June 5	59
1:10 p.m. June 5	64
3:30 p.m. June 5	80
Moments Before, One Hundred Fifty Miles West of the Hawaiian Islands	81
4:10 p.m. June 5	86
MEANWHILE	95
6:55 p.m. June 5	103
7:41 p.m. June 5	107
9:49 p.m. June 5	113
2:20 a.m. June 6	116
MEANWHILE 28 MILES AWAY	120
6:07 a.m. June 6	122
Back Aboard the *Blue Pelican*	130
8:29 a.m. June 6	132
9:51 a.m. June 6	140
10:03 a.m. June 6	141
10:14 a.m. June 6	143
10:29 a.m. June 6	144
10:54 a.m. June 6	149
10:59 a.m. June 6	151
11:04 a.m. June 6	153

11:17 a.m. June 6	157
11:26 a.m. June 6	159
11:33 a.m. June 6	161
6:11 p.m. June 7	165
About the Author	169

PREFACE

One night I experienced a dream about the enclosed story. I thought it unique, but soon forgot it. Nine days later the same dream reoccurred. Thinking it was coincidental I promptly dismissed it again.

Three days later I experienced the same dream, but with a more intensity and detail. Something was different this time. The words were crying to be let out. *Something* or *someone* was urging me to get this down on paper. I fought the urge, thinking it was my own mind driving me, however, I soon learned I would find no rest until I did.

Herein you will find an intriguing story about three men who shared the same congruent dreams about a lone survivor, a new born, still alive in the hull of a sunken liner. What happens next becomes an adventure against time.

This is a story that's never been told. It has the reader moving from page to page, anxiously awaiting what will happen next. See if you can spot the clues along the way that ties everything together in the final chapter. Maybe dreams do come true.

Never laugh at anyone's dreams. People who don't have dreams don't have much.

11:26 p.m. June 1

"Whaaagh."

Chris strained to pull himself awake. Although asleep, he knew he was *entering* the same terrifying dream he had experienced over the past several weeks. They always began with a baby crying somewhere in the dark, but soon progressed into fear-gripping nightmares. As he sank deeper into sleep, he found himself at the bottom of the ocean. In front of him was what he thought to be a recently sunken ocean liner. He reasoned it was recent, as there were no signs of the iron-eating microorganism called Rusticle, which is the first to move in on a relic. An eel had taken refuge in one of the scuppers and fish were only beginning to use it as safety against predators. In the distance, he could hear a baby crying. Suddenly he found himself moving down a passageway, searching each compartment furiously, even managing to gash his thigh on jagged steel, as he hastily worked his way down the corridor. The crying grew louder. He moved nearer until he approached a door, where he instinctively knew the child would be found. His heart was racing with expectation.

Chris put his weight against the door. As it reluctantly gave way, a bright luminescent light shone from within. He sheltered his eyes while attempting to see from where it was coming. As his eyes adjusted, he could see the room was nearly full of water with only a two-foot air pocket left, which was slowly filling, with water. Gazing at the sight before him, he made a sound in the back of his throat, as he tried to take in what could only be impossible. Above the water was a pair of hands holding a crying infant, which appeared to be only a few days old. The blackish umbilical cord was still attached. Its skin had become red from crying, turning the birthmark on its thigh purple. The hands were slowly sinking beneath the water, taking the child with them. Looking below and above the water Chris blinked, looked puzzled, and tilted his head as if it would help him understand what he was witnessing. He was transfixed and horrified. His mind did not realize the full paradox of what his eyes were seeing. Fear clutched at his throat, and held it as he struggled to see who was supporting the child. Disbelieving, again he looked below the water. No one was there—-they were *disembodied hands.* 'I don't believe this,' he thought to himself. Reason parted company with his brain as he ransacked it for a logical explanation. His heart was pounding in his ears as he tried to quiet the fear rising within. Soon the room would be filled with water, and the child would be lost forever. Desperate to escape this impossibility, he wanted to turn and run. He shrank back, his legs felt like cement and his heart thumped wildly. His bladder released its contents. The taste of adrenaline flooded his mouth.

Suddenly a vision appeared close to the ceiling. As quickly as he had panicked, he had become calm. It was the face of a woman he thought he had known somewhere deep in the past. Each detail stood out with merciless clarity in the bright light. Her long, red hair flowed in an invisible breeze. The luminescent light emanating from her gave her a ghostly, yet saintly appearance. Her green eyes shone like emeralds while they mirrored the anguish she must have been feeling. "Save my child," she pleaded, "save her. There's so little time."

He realized she must have been the mother. Feeling her pain, he wanted to comfort her, yet out of fear, said nothing. She lingered for a few moments, still speaking to him, but with words he could not discern. Then the image began to fade, leaving only the faint fragrance of roses.

When Chris looked back, the baby was being held by one of the hands, while the other gestured him forward, urging him to take the tiny child. As he reached for the infant, he was suddenly bolted awake.

The dream was so realistic, so terrifying, that when he woke, he was shaking; beads of sweat covered his brow. Sucking air, he tried to slow his breathing, but his chest throbbed as though he had been fighting for air. The dreams were so vivid, so real, yet always ended abruptly at the same place. Something very frightening was going on.

Gasping, he listened, his pupils wide in the dark. The child's heart-rending cries had stopped. The room was quiet. There was only the sound of light traffic outside his window and the gentle roll of the waves.

In his attempt to purge himself of the dream he asked himself why he was having the same ones over and over. Was his subconscious trying to tell him something? Was he just worn out?

Chris studied at Vanderbilt University where he received his Ph.D. in Meteorology and with the Scripps Institute of Oceanography in La Jolla, CA, where he received his Ph.D. in Oceanography. He then served in the U.S. Navy where he honed his skills in both fields. He was officer-in-charge of Underwater Exploration for lost and sunken vessels, and a consultant in matters relating to underwater exploration, with other branches of the service. After twelve years of service he was offered, and accepted, a job with the <u>National Oceanic and Atmospheric Administration</u> located in Honolulu, Hawaii, on the island of Oahu.

Hours were long, with frequent travel crisscrossing the oceans, various speaking engagements, and too few days off. *Yeah*, he thought, *that's it. Water...sinking to the bottom...a wreck...maybe it's my subconscious trying to tell me I'm losing it. What about the crying baby? How did that fit in? Who was the woman? Where had he seen her before?* Exhausted, Chris gave up looking for answers and shrugged it off as another nightmare.

As he laid in the dark, his mind continued having an ongoing conversation with itself. A part of it tried to convince him that it was the job that was encroaching upon his sleep. *It's only a dream. From beginning to end, it's only a dream; just a bad dream...I'm just working too hard*, but his gut wasn't buying any of it. The other side repeated over and over to itself, what *if this is a message, an omen? What if it's real? What if there is a real child trapped somewhere.*

He was lucky to find this bungalow within a short distance of work. When he first arrived, he stayed with Cuppy in his one bedroom apartment. After several weeks of putting up with his snoring, he heard a colleague was looking for a house sitter while he visited the mainland. Several months later he decided to stay in the states, and offered to rent the place to him until his return, if ever. That was four and a half years ago.

The house was constructed in the early forties with one bedroom, one bath, a tiny kitchen, and a small living room with a wonderful nook, which he used as an office. Rattan furniture graced the living room along with the recliner, which occupied a prized place in front of the TV. The chair was broken in from years of use and since he would never part with it, so he had it shipped over from the mainland when he took this job. Books and magazines lay strewn about the house, but always within easy reach, no matter where he lit. The sheer curtains hanging from the large window that faced the ocean were beginning to dry rot from the sun. He considered purchasing new ones, but thought shopping was 'woman stuff'. He made a mental note to mention them to Sky, the love of his life. Maybe she would take the hint and purchase some new ones. He hated shopping.

Various framed pictures of his family sat on two end tables with three or four more hanging in the hall, along with degrees and awards he had earned. One was a photograph of two men in uniform with their arms draped around each other. They held his brothers frozen in time. Their closely spaced deaths in Vietnam had devastated him. Two others displayed two of his three sisters on their wedding days. Both married farmers, and to this day, continue to reside close to their parents. The third sister married as soon as she was eighteen and moved to Mexico City. Another silver-framed picture was of his parents on their wedding day, which was beginning to fade to brown. Still another was a snapshot of Chris with his parents when he was four years old. His mother was holding a baby, but he had never thought too much about it. It was about that time his aunt had recently visited them with new a baby girl. He assumed it was her child.

Chris Healey was born in rural area of Poplar, IL to Marion and Charles Healey, a poor tenant farmer, forty-three years ago. His great grandparents had settled the quarter acre section, where they lived, over a century ago. By the time the guardians of the land learned about rotating crops and resting the land, it was too late for his father to eke a living out of the fallow ground. The damage could not be undone. For years they lived on too little funds from county welfare.

Life was a constant struggle for the family. Chris, the youngest of six children, was oblivious to the problems facing his parents. In those earlier years the only thing he remembered clearly was his mother bursting into tears, for no apparent reason. She would hold his tiny body tight to her breast, almost smothering him, as she cried.

Out, "What have I done? What have I done?" Eventually his father would come in to comfort her.

"You ain't done nothin' momma, nothin'…only what ya had to do. Everything is okay. Ya know everything is okay. Now don't cry momma. Come on; let's go for a walk.

Chris would wait anxiously for their return because it meant his momma would be smiling again.

The only body of water Chris had ever seen, until he was eight years old, was a small pond 50 meters outside their back door. In-between waiting for the monthly welfare check and drinking with 'the boys,' his dad took his sons fishing. Although the pond could not

Three Dreams

support life, they had fun pretending to catch the 'big one' anyway. Sometimes they would snare a toad or two and would have 'meat' on the table that night. Chris usually found himself smiling when he recalled those days.

Once, their state check arrived with four extra dollars added in. With it, his father took the family to the County Fair in a nearby town. After cotton candy and tossing pennies for a big prize, Chris wandered over a hill to discover, to his awe, the Spoon River. It would be here that he first fell in love with diving.

While standing on a small pier overlooking the river, he was startled out of his wits when, two divers suddenly popped out of the water. With seeing their black wet suits, he thought they were monsters from the deep. A film of tears brimmed his eyes as he screeched for his dad. Trembling, he was on the edge of unruly panic. Hearing the terror in his son's voice, his dad came running. When he learned what had happened, he and the divers tried, unsuccessfully, to stifle their amusement. Chris wanted to run and hide. With no TV growing up, how could he have known? He had never seen a wet suit before, much less divers.

The two men tried to redeem themselves by offering to take him on a dive the very next day. He could hardly wait and lay awake that night imagining what he'd find; sea monsters, dinosaur-like fish, mermaids, or maybe even sunken treasure. He already had it planned how he'd spend the money if he found treasure chests full of gold. First he'd buy a puppy, then, then buy his mom and dad a house, then a bicycle for all his sisters and brothers, and then ….

Unable to contain his son's excitement, he and Chris arrived two hours early the next morning. When the divers arrived Chris followed their instructions with close attention and was soon under water. Gripping his arms firmly as they swam, they showed him the wonders of underwater life. He thought his heart would burst through his chest with the thrill and wanted to stay down there forever. The 20-minute dive was an awesome adventure of search and discovery. Although in the water a short time, it was enough to kindle the fires of ambition for the sea, forever. Since he was an extraordinary bright child, it was no surprise to his parents when, at the age of 12, he announced he wanted to become an underwater archeologist.

Luckily, after graduating high school, through an endowment plan, he was able to follow his dreams, much to the pride of his parents. He was the first from every generation to go to College.

Chris burrowed into his pillow, closed his eyes and tried to will a dreamless sleep. Soft music flowed in his window from a hidden source. His mind urged him to find a logical reason for these crazy dreams. Tossing and turning he gave up trying to sleep and propped himself up on his pillows. He watched the soft balmy breeze gently billow the curtains. The subdued lighting cast shadows across his small bungalow room. They danced across the room to the glass framed obsolete diving suit hanging on the wall that Cuppy had given him on his birthday two years ago. Contained within were the 30-pound dive boots, an 80-pound weight belt, a rubberized canvas body suit, 29-pound breastplate, and the dated detachable 54-pound brass helmet. He recalled with delight the day he had come home to find the Jules Verne regalia already hanging on the wall. Cuppy rarely gave gifts, but he outdid himself with this one. Looking around he thought it was easily the most attractive piece in the room. The dancing light seemed to give it life. Although antiquated Chris prized this treasure more than any other, because it reminded him of his first meeting with Cuppy.

His hand fell to the ache in his thigh. He didn't notice the trickle of blood falling in droplets upon the sheet.

His mind drifted over to Cuppy. He chuckled as he reminisced of the time he met him, thirteen years ago. Then, Chris loved living on the brink, thinking he was infallible. He joined another diving class thinking he could push the envelope a little further. Cuppy was his designated diving instructor. He had read a great deal about, and was fascinated with, submerged remains of earlier civilizations and speculated about the men who had sailed them and their last moments before they went down.

An intriguing wreck nearby was beckoning him. After only four hours in lessons in underwater navigational skills in wreck diving, Chris foolishly decided to explore an old maritime relic on his own, although he knew diving was not a loner sport. It was too dangerous but Chris wasn't worried…danger was his aphrodisiac. At twenty-five he believed he was immortal and arrogantly thought he knew everything there was to know about the oceans and skin diving.

As he explored the deep green fantasyland he was unaware the thick blanket of kelp that covered the wreck was becoming entangled with his tanks. With stealth, the giant algae, which grew like forests about the wreck, wrapped their stipes and fronds around his only connection to life, as he maneuvered about in his investigation. Only when he started to ascend, did he realize the predicament that had befallen him. Struggling, panic began to set in. He fought with the giants of the deep, to no avail. The more he struggled, the tighter the grip the Goliath's held on him, and his cylinders.

Suddenly Cuppy and a buddy diver were there, chopping away at the mammoth shoots. Chris could see the muscles standing out in his tight-set jaw as Cuppy eyed him with a menacing glare. The repetition of his rescuer's warning…*the importance of the buddy system cannot be overestimated*, came back to haunt him. Cuppy was not a happy man.

Soon they were top side. Feeling foolish, Chris says,"You saved my life down there."

"Yes, I know." He said matter-of-factly, not looking at him.

There was much to be said, but neither one of them said another word, and never mentioned the incident again.

It was then that a lasting bond was established. Neither could have known that their bonds of friendship were forged forever in that rescue. The two men seemed to take to each other after just as if nothing had ever happened and have been together ever since.

Roberta M. Alleman

7:45 a.m. June 2

The warm penetrating sunlight pouring through the open windows awoke Chris early the following morning. A light breeze emanated a soothing floral fragrance through the curtains that were still blowing in endless undulation. He sprang out of bed and gave a shivering all over stretch. *Ah, I feel good*, he thought as he yawned and twisted, not giving any thought to his dream. He reached down to rub the ache in his thigh. Feeling dried blood he twisted to look down to find a gash about three inches long, with the surrounding skin the color of eggplant. Curious, he pulled back the covers, to discover a bloodstain where he had slept. *Guess I really gouged myself good*, he thought. Suddenly a flash from the dream appeared. He saw where he had gashed his leg on the jagged steel. The image disappeared as quickly as it came. Still, he rationalized it was only a scratch he had given himself during the night.

Looking at his watch he wondered when Sky would call. He had left strict instructions with his team not to call him on his day off, with penalty of being beheaded.

The phone rang.

Grabbing his robe he lifted the receiver, "What," he snapped as he struggled to push his arm through the sleeve.

"Excuse me. Did we get out of bed on the wrong side this morning," the voice asked. It was Sky.

"Sorry, I thought it might be the office. I'm glad it's you. Where are you?"

"Had breakfast yet?" Her voice was like music to his ears. *What a great way to start the day*, he thought.

"Not yet, but I'm hungry for you."

"I'm at Kate's place," she chuckled, exuding the same bubbling enthusiasm she always had. "Already ordered, so put the coffee on. You **do** have coffee, don't you? Be there in five."

"It'll be ready. Hurry up hon."

Hastily he threw on a jersey and jeans, shaved, doused his face and neck with after shave lotion, combed his hair and finished by spraying room deodorant throughout the place.

Three Dreams

Chris smiled to himself. Although he worked every day along side of Sky, he always felt good when he could spend quality time with her. She was not a raving beauty but had an inner quality that kept him coming back for more. He'd kid her about her coming from Switzerland because of her hazel eyes and blonde hair, which set off her peachy outdoorsy complexion. "Just like out of a Swiss poster," he'd kid her. "I'm just a southern peach," she'd drawl back, but in reality, she was born in Boston.

When he first met Sky Darby he didn't trust women. Even though he was considered the area's most coveted bachelor, he wouldn't let any particular woman get close to him, but Sky was different. They became a couple four months after she joined the <u>National Oceanic and Atmospheric Administration</u>. Both felt they hadn't had time for marriage, but if they ever did settle down, it would be with each other. He loved her laughter, her sense of humor, and the way she wiggled her nose to keep her glasses up, and, of course, her gorgeous kissable lips. Although they were separated by their identities they were joined by their love for each other. He felt almost immoral about lusting after her, but there was something so exotic, so sensual, and yet delicate about her that touched both the animal and the protective sides of him. He wondered what she ever saw in him. She could have anyone at her beck and call—and she did. The thought of her with another aroused the green-eyed monster within. Wherever she went she was the focus of a roomful of people, but carried herself as though she wasn't aware of the effect she had on others. The rare quality of vulnerability and sophistication coupled with her self-assured dignity gave some the impression she might be a snob, but she was quiet, sensitive, conscientious, patient and funny. Initially, he ignored her when she joined the team, thinking he hadn't a chance, but here they were, together, four years later.

Sky was his rock...the perfect antidote for his complexities. Without her sound advice and unflagging support, these past four years, Chris would probably still not trust women.

A knock came at the door.

"Ah, food at last," he says as he flung open the door.

"You expecting a pizza delivery or somethin'," asked Cuppy, as he reluctantly entered. He was dressed in a casual navy blue shirt, jeans, Rebocks, and was sock less. His hair, per usual, was neatly combed but looked like it needed a trim. His practically unlined face was always red, giving him a 'Santa Clause' complexion, which was complimented by his fashionably gray hair, eyebrows and sideburns…all he lacked was the beard! Thinking eyeglasses made him look too old, he religiously wore contacts when out in public.

"No, just Sky. She's bringing over breakfast and we're *both* going to sit down, *alone,* and eat it right here, by ourselves. Got it?"

"I'm not here to bother you." He turned to face him. "I know it's your day off…it's just that…that Scott's in trouble. He and his old lady had been at it again. Leo called from the *Blue Swan* and said if we didn't come'n git him that he's gonna call the cops." He grinned nervously.

"What's he done now?"

"I'll let Leo tell you. It's too weird. All I can tell you is that he's drunk and lookin' for trouble."

Chris spoke quietly, barely concealing his anger. "For pity sakes couldn't you get him yourself? What do you need me for?"

"Because somethin' is goin' on that I think you should know about," he says firmly. He shoved his hands into his pockets and dug at the carpet with the toe of his sneaker, moving an imaginary object.

"What's the mystery? What's so important that it can't wait?" Chris moved toward the kitchen. As he filled the coffeepot with water he glanced at his watch, impatient that Sky wasn't here to rescue him. It was his day off and he didn't want to go anywhere.

Somber and looking down at his feet Cuppy asked, "What would you say if I told you he had one of those baby dreams?"

Chris's mind raced with anticipation at his next words. His expression didn't change but he was listening intently.

"So what does that mean? So he dreamed about a baby…there's nothing spectacular about that…" he says without looking up. The hairs on the back of his neck and arms stood up. He never told Scott about his dreams. First, he didn't think he'd understand, and second, he'd have it all over the office in a day.

"What if…what if. I told you it's…it's not the first," he asked as he peeked around the corner at Chris, watching for a reaction.

"That's not funny Cup," he says. He knew Cuppy wouldn't kid about something like this. Although he didn't say it, he knew he was concerned too.

Cuppy, an only child, was born Cuppani Bachmeir in Germany at the onset of the war. His family frequently hid Jews before the underground could arrange to take them across the border into Switzerland. Although very young during those terrible years, he learned how to keep secrets and when to keep quiet. His family was eventually caught, and promptly shot, while he watched from his hiding place in a neighbor's rafters. He lived with relatives until, in his teens, he migrated to England where he learned to dive when he held odd jobs with an underwater salvage company. Eventually he joined the British navy where he taught others deep sea diving. That is where he met his most memorable student, Chris. He was a stele of a man who radiated irresistible charm and was said to be kindred to a Teddy Bear. He was well known, respected, loved and could pull more strings, if you were a friend, than a puppeteer. He carried his large frame well on his six-foot body and was the most sought after diver on the islands. There wasn't a cringe in him anywhere. Nobody intimidated him. If anything, it was the other way around. There was nothing disconnected about anything he said or did. His roller coaster laugh was so infectious that one would find themselves laughing along with him, even if he didn't want to.

Since he lived a few blocks away, he would stop in on his way home to visit whenever he saw Chris' car in the driveway. He'd always bring a six-pack and would hang around for a few hours. At times Chris found himself parking in the rear.

Cuppy slowly entered the kitchen, leaned against the counter and fiddled with a loose thread attached to a buttonhole. "I'm only tellin' you what Leo told me, ole buddy," he said into his chest.

Chris hated it when he called him 'ole buddy'. He knew he was trying to protect him from something or someone when he called him that. He trusted him enough to tell only Cuppy and, of course Sky, of his dreams. They initially had a few laughs over it, but eventually the humor waned. Chris wasn't aware, but Cuppy had already pulled some strings and had asked friends to investigate these phenomena because he could see the changes in his friend since the onset of the dreams. He had become temperamental and impatient, whereas, previously he was easy going. He was as equally perplexed and wanted to get to the bottom of it.

Maybe Scott tuned into my dreams; after all, he does have some clairvoyance. No, no it can't be that, thought Chris.

"Are you sure that's what he said? A dream...a baby," he asked as indifferently as possible. He felt a flutter of apprehension and excitement.

A thousand years later he answered, "Yup!" Cuppy nodded deliberately.

Just then Sky entered the open door with their breakfast cradled in one arm and an overnight bag slung over the opposite shoulder. The close fitting jeans and red-checkered shirt showed her figure without looking cheap. Although she wore running shoes, she was sure that wasn't exactly what Chris had in mind for the day.

"I'm here," she called, "are you hot to trot?"

Not seeing Chris, she moved toward the kitchen. It took a second for it to register that someone else was present. Sky straightened noticeably when she saw Cuppy. She sighed unhappily. To control her displeasure she remained furiously silent. Although she loved Cuppy, and he was a long time friend, it was rare when she and Chris could be alone without him dropping by. She eyed him sideways as she placed the Styrofoam cartons on the counter. Right now she didn't care that he was Chris's best friend and reproached herself for resenting him. Time alone with Chris, with no emergencies or interruptions, was all she wanted. She did love Cuppy for one thing though; he worshiped the ground Chris walked on.

"Okay Cuppy, what's it this time? Are you coming or going? Sorry, there's not enough for three." It was evident that she was upset with his presence, due to the coldness with which she spoke. She added with undisguised distaste, "Why don't you go over to Kate's? They serve a great breakfast there." *He must think my understanding is elastic, capable of stretching at will, and to any lengths, when it comes to his friendship with Chris,* she thought. *Well, what about me?*

The atmosphere was brittle but still within the bounds of civility.

Embarrassed, Cuppy reddened. He lowered his head and jabbed his thumb in Chris's direction.

There was a long terminal pause before Chris got the message and relayed their conversation about Scott. Sky knew instinctively that breakfast was off—-again—- before he got half way through. She also knew Chris had to resolve any questions he may have, before he could relax for the day. Perhaps they'd have time later. It was either stay here by herself and breakfast alone, or go along with them. She grabbed three pieces of toast from the box and headed for the door. "Let's go," she said in resignation. Her stomach grumbled in protest.

Although she understood his need to go, she could never share in it. She concluded long ago that they were only transient.

He was pleased Sky didn't make a fuss—-she had every right to. Their last three get-togethers were disastrous, but he could not stop himself, he had to know.

Going out the door Cuppy says, "Oh yes, there's another guy there who claims the same thing."

"Same what?"

"Same dreams, ole buddy."

"Are you shitting me?" Chris waited for details. He gave none.

Cuppy was walking ahead and didn't answer him.

Roberta M. Alleman

9:04 a.m. June 02

For the past thirty years the Southwestern-inspired style bar, the Blue Swan, sat modestly on the corners of Kawaiaha'o and South Street. From this location, melodies of ancient chants would frequently emanate from luaus on the beach, which sometimes, was a refreshing break from Leo's Frank Sinatra's records.

As they entered, their eyes took in the murky room. The aroma of freshly cooked ribs, mixed with a faint scent of ammonia, filled the air. Chris turned and looked around the room slowly. The 55-foot by 28-foot cocktail lounge was a mixture of upscale billiards and sports bar, with antique guns, ropes, saddles and other memorabilia from the early west, adorning the walls. The J shaped bar sat to the left with 3 billiard tables in the rear. Against the center rear wall was a stage with a large silent TV propped on a table. The once brightly painted walls now gave off a yellowish hue from the many years of cigarette smoke. The glassed-in view of the attached gleaming kitchen, and of which cuisine was cooking next door, offered the customers mild entertainment while they leisurely sipped their favorite drinks. Their specialty was baby back ribs and BBQ chicken, which Cuppy would usually order the minute he came in. Since food was passed through a window that connected the two, the aromas that percolated through kept their chefs busy until the bar closed at 1:00 a.m.

Moving toward Scott, they crossed a floor where crushed empty cigarette packs, popcorn, cigarette butts, and other unrecognizable debris laid strewn about like fallen leaves. Wisps of blue smoke made lazy circles above their heads. Two customers sat at the bar, with a few others scattered at the tables. Most were oblivious to their arrival. The smell of the food stabbed Sky's hungry stomach like a knife.

Nothing was said as they closed the distance toward Scott. His deep breathing, coupled with the drool running down the side of his face onto his sleeve, made it was clear he was passed out.

"Hey Leo! How much you give 'im to get 'im that way," Cuppy asked, ducking his head to peer into Scott's face. He and Scott maintained and uneasy truce for Chris's sake, but wouldn't have anything to do with each other otherwise.

Leo's face took on a strange look, as if he'd bitten into something he didn't know if he liked or not. His eyes widened and his posture tightened as he waggled his finger in Cuppy's direction.

"Oh no, don't lay that on me! He was pretty far-gone when he got here. I just gave him one Cava Cava. That's when he was ranting about his wife and some dream he had. Said she couldn't keep a secret. Ha, he should talk. Then he was mumbling about a baby in a dream and how he had to save it...well...something like that. I couldn't make heads nor tails of it ...sounds like a whopper to me. He's tells some good ones sometimes. Yeah, a baby in a sunken remnant of a ship," he laughed. "And that's not all. The best is yet to come. See that guy over there...the one with bib overalls," he asked, pointing his finger toward the three men sitting at a table across the room. "That one told him what was in his dream without Scott hardly sayin' nothin'. Scott got pissed and starting raving about his big mouth wife telling everyone. The guy was tellin' him that *he* had the same dream but Scott wasn't listening. Kept calling him a liar. Said he knew Marlene had blabbed it all over cuz she was tryin' to get back at him. Thought the guy was makin' fun of him. The bloke told him he didn't know no Marlene but Scott just kept shouting at him anyway. I told the both of 'em they could get the hell out if they didn't sit down and act like gentlemen. Scott sat down where he is now and promptly passed out. I can't have that going on in my bar. Give this place a bad name." His laugh was all over the place.

Chris eyed the three men. Casually he asked, "Who are they? Where'd they come from? I don't remember seeing them here before."

"They usually hang out at the *Sea Gull* but the cops closed it for too many violations. They work on the trawlers at the wharf. Been comin' here last couple-a-weeks. Nice blokes. Don't give me any trouble. Need a few more like 'em in here"

Leo knew everything about everybody. He worked as the bartender since the doors opened 30 years ago. Although 60 and a large man, he could maneuver gracefully among the tables, as well, if not better, than a young waitress could. His reddish blonde handlebar mustache and red cheeks led one to believe he was Irish. Truly, he was Polish, but would never discourage anyone from believing he was Irish. He thought it more prestigious to be Irish than a Pollock. He had a remarkable capacity for friendship and on every St. Patrick's Day he'd throw a large party for his friends and customers with free food and booze. Although he didn't drink, he would have a few with his friends only on St. Patty's.

Chris was stunned. Was it true? Did they all have the same dreams? Impossible! The possibility both excited and frightened him. He needed a plan to get the man's confidence. He plunked himself into a stool with his back facing the room. Directly in front of him was a large golden-framed mirror. Through it his eyes were riveted on the men who were almost hidden by an artificial plant. Two other empty tables flanked them. Frowning, he crossed his arms across his chest, moved uncomfortably in his seat, and contemplated how he could question the seaman without sounding like a fool. Obeying an impulse, he turned toward the men.

"Leo...Give those men a round on me," he says without taking his eyes off them. He hoped the men would invite him over to join them. It was obvious he wasn't going to get anything out of Scott right now anyway.

Leo prepared their drinks and navigated around the tables, almost as if he were on skates. Without a word he served the drinks, then leaning down, he said something to one of the men, pointed toward Chris, then headed back to the bar. The men glimpsed at him briefly. Leo returned, shrugged his shoulders, and proceeded to wash glasses.

Sky gave Chris a level stare. It was like she wasn't even there. Realizing it wouldn't do any good to say anything; she swallowed her resentment and resigned herself that this was going to take a while. Retreating to the safety of silence, she ordered an Irish coffee and settled back.

Chris waited. Nothing happened. The only sound he heard was the pounding in his own chest. Trying to appear relaxed, he slumped in his chair and laced his fingers across his chest. All the while he was observing the three men through the mirror.

After a few anxious minutes he decided to walk over to their table. A thousand questions raced through his mind as he crossed the room. Who was this man? What role did he play in this? What was the connection? Did he really have the same dreams, and if so, are there others? He needed answers.

No one looked up when he approached.

Chris found the nerve to speak. "I understand you guys work at the harbor."

He waited for a response. Nothing. He went on, "My grandfather used to work aboard the *Loni Lai.*" They stared at him, coldly, expressionless. "Loved that old tug," he continued, pulling up a chair and straddling it. "Worked on her till he died. Used to talk about her all the time. She was his mistress," he smiled in an insincere way. "Perhaps you knew him...Barney, Barney Healey. Everyone called him Barnacle. I'm Chris Healey, Dr. Chris Healey.

"Gawd, a doctor yet," remarked one man, sarcastically eyeing him through the smoke. His face almost looked ophidian.

"Do tell," bleated the second, looking at Chris dubiously over his shoulder. His face, a grid of lines, traced his history in the sun.

"Barnacle Barney? You his grandson? I sailed with him many a time," said the third man, loudly. "That man could smell them fish 10 miles away. Never knew anything like it. I could tell you some stories about your grand pappy and the old days together." He threw his head back and laughed deeply. Recovering from his private joke, he introduced his two companions. "This here's Lucky ...called that 'cause he ain't dead yet...taint his real name. Almost drown three times Yup, fished him out of the waters three times...only survivor twice. Right Lucky?"

Lucky stopped tamping the tobacco into his pipe and reached out a gnarled hand that looked like an old leather baseball mitt in the vague image of a hand. His firm grasp surpassed that of a man of his 57 years. He appeared to be of Scandinavian heritage because of his white hair, and blonde eyebrows, which connected across the bridge of his nose. His eyes were wide set with blonde, almost feminine eyelashes, giving him the semblance of an albino. When he smiled his teeth, while perfect, Chris believed to be his own. "Howdy," he said softly. Surrounding the faint smile were chapped and cracking lips.

Looks painful, Chris thought.

"That's Lou... Lou Davis. He's our inventor. You should see some of the things he's invented...be rich some day, he will. He has insights into things that none of us do but he can't tell ya where to catch them big ones. Ain't himself today. Got the jitters, ain't ya Lou," he says laughing, elbowing him in the ribs. "A few drinks ought ta settle ya down."

Lou remained hunched over his drink nervously fingering the cigarette pack before him. His graying hair was pulled back in a ponytail and looked like it needed washing. The bib overalls he wore reeked of fish, cigarettes, and various other sundries. He forced a slight smile, with a spike in it. He shook hands with Chris just complaisant enough for Chris to feel the thoroughness of his skin and the hard-thickened calluses on his fingers and palm. Dark circles ringed his eyes that were overshadowed by his graying eyebrows. Even with his leathery skin there was something about this man that instinctively told Chris there was something different about him. He couldn't put his finger on it but he felt an intense connection.

"Howdy," Chris says.

"I'm called D.C. and I ain't tellin' ya why I got that handle," he chuckled. "You work with the sea too, doc?"

"In a way. I kind of watch the sea. I work with the Oceanic and Atmosphere Administration," Chris replies, taking a long hungry look at Lou. He was itching to jump in and start asking him questions.

"I know all about them. Read it in the *National Geographic*. You guys tell us when dem giant waves are comin," D.C. says proudly, nodding to his friends.

"They're called Tsunami."

"St...what?"

"Tsunami...giant waves...seismic sea waves. They're generated by underwater earthquakes around the margins of the Pacific Ocean and can travel up to 600 miles an hour."

"How come I ain't ever seen one? I've been on the sea most of my life and I ain't seen none."

"Because the waves are only two to three feet high in the open ocean. It's only when they reach land that they're known as Tsunami. Some die out, some reach lands only a few feet high. On rare occasions they're tidal waves, or Tsunamis, and can become as much as 60 feet high, or more.

"How'd you know when they're comin'?"

Chris was growing impatient. He didn't want to talk about Tsunamis or anything else. He wanted to interrogate Lou about his dreams. He wanted to find out if it was true what Leo had told him...that he had had the same dreams. He thought of how pathetically ridiculous he would appear if he were wrong, if Lou hadn't experienced any dreams at all.

Not wanting to ruffle any feathers, he continued. "We have sophisticated equipment that tell us of any changes in the earth's crust, earthquakes being one of them, volcano eruptions, another.

You've probably heard of the Seismograph. That's just one method we use," he said with pained patience.

Now was his chance. "Say Lou, Leo tells me you got into it with that guy over there at the bar…the one that's passed out. What was that all about?

"Ya, ya…he and Lou really went a few rounds. He was only trying to tell him he understood about the dreams. Been havin' them himself," D.C. responded, throwing up his hands, miming disgust.

"What do you mean dreams? What kind of dreams," he asked cautiously, fishing.

Lou shook his head. His dreams both scared, and intrigued him. He didn't want Chris to think he'd lost it so he remained quiet and continued fumbling with the cigarette pack. Music emanated from the jukebox. Strangely it was "What Kind of Fool am I," by Sammy Davis Jr., one of Leo's favorite.

"Lou's been having some dreams that's bugging him. He wakes up in a sweat or yelling about some baby. He's gettin' to be a real pain. Gonna sleep on deck if he doesn't knock it off. I gotta get some sleep." At one point Lucky had left the table to get some beers.

Chris stared at Lou, waiting for him to add something to D.C.'s explanation. Nothing. He contemplated whether he should tell him first of his own experience. He wanted to talk to someone about this, someone who might understand, and, perhaps have some answers. He swallowed hard, took a swig of his drink and decided to take a chance.

He moved close to Lou's ear. "You're dreaming. In the dream you heard a baby crying… just crying, in the beginning. Next, you find yourself underwater and you see a sunken vessel lying there on its side. You search for the crying child within the ship. Your mind tells you this can't be so, but perhaps a miracle has happened, and it has survived, maybe within an air pocket or something. It doesn't seem rational, but you've *got* to push on. Your mind tells you you're dreaming and you try to wake up, but you can't. To push forward is the stronger impulse."

Lou's eyes were becoming as large as saucers. He nodded, smiling behind those tortured lips. His head bobbed up and down in agreement. His attention had left the cigarette pack and gone to Chris. "Yeah, yeah," he says enthusiastically, turning in his seat to face him. "I thought I was going nuts but…how…."

Chris interrupted "You find yourself searching one cabin after another until finally, you know you're at the right one."

"Yeah, and that's when I wake up. I can never get inside but I can hear this...this crying," Lou responds.

Encouraged because Lou's dreams were congruent with his, Chris pushed on, wondering for a moment, why he had gotten beyond the door, but Lou hadn't. "And when you wake up you feel like you've almost drowned. You gasp for air; you're sweating profusely, sometimes even screaming.

"Yeah, that's it. That's exactly it. Why? What's going on? What..." his mouth dropped, too astonished to speak.

"You think maybe you're losing it or maybe it's from your own making." Lou looked, to his astonishment, like he was about to cry. Startled, the men stared at each other in disbelief, then stared at Chris, with rapt attention. Their questioning eyes fixed on him.

"You *think* you're going crazy because it happens again and again, and you're afraid to tell anyone because they'll think you're nuts," He pounded his fist sharply on the table. "Well you're not...I've had them too. I've had..." Chris trailed off. Remembering the dreams, they unfolded before him, not according to coherent logic, but rather with the foreboding whimsy of a nightmare.

Each man was lost in his own thoughts, trying to make some sense of the whole thing. On one hand they both experienced the same dreams—-up to a point. On the other hand, a child still alive somewhere in a sunken ship? Incredulous! Impossible! Preposterous! Then again, stranger things have happened.

Lucky, feeling contemptuous remained aloof and silent throughout most of the unsolicited narration. Midway through he recognized some points that Lou had offhandedly told him earlier. Soon his interest was peaking.

"And what about that guy," Lou asked soberly, jerking his head toward the bar where Scott sat, still passed out. "What about him? What does he say?"

"I'm afraid I haven't had a chance to talk to him yet. I just heard about both of you today. You say he told you he had the dreams too?"

"Well, he did not exactly *tell* me. He was ranting about them off and on. I recognized the story. Been there. When I tried to ask him about it, he blew. Thought his old lady had been tellin' everyone...that I was makin' fun of him. Wanted to come to fisticuffs over it. He didn't have a chance 'cuz I could see he was too drunk, and besides, I don't get into bar fights.

Chris, now, more than ever, wanted to get to the bottom of this. He thought of an old friend he went to school with, who might be able to help him. The conversation continued for another twenty minutes, until he remembered he had left Sky and Cuppy at the bar. Before departing they exchanged numbers promising to contact each other.

When he stood to return to the bar he was surprised to find that his knees felt weak.

D.C. stood and reached out his hand. "Thanks Mate." He slapped Chris on the back as he turned to leave. Chris willed his legs to move. As he moved away, he heard him say, "Wouldn't it be real funny if it turned out to be true? Wouldn't that be somethin' now?" No one was laughing.

As he approached the bar, Chris could see Scott was just starting to come to. He was supporting his head between his two hands while Sky held a cold towel to the back of his neck. Saliva, that was now dried, had run down his chin, leaving a white chalky line cuff. Sky offered him a bar napkin and suggested he wipe his face.

Scott Spencer was now 44. At a very young age he accepted his clairvoyance as an every day occurrence. He thought everyone had the ability to see things before they happened. As he grew older and related some of these experiences to his parents, they became afraid and thought they were acts of the devil. They were well along in years when he was born, were poor, uneducated and lived in the Blue Ridge Mountains of Virginia. Neither his parents nor the local community understood his God given gift. After years of being denied and told he was touched by the devil, Scott began keeping his abilities to himself. It was when he foresaw death, often weeks before it happened, that he would find solace in alcohol. The visions terrified him. Believing he was possessed, he spent the rest of his life running from his talent.

His father was strict and ran his home and family like a boot camp. He wanted his son to go to the best schools, take the hardest subjects, and "make something of himself. "Excel, excel, excel…only then can you make something of yourself," he would say over and over again. Nothing Scott did would please him even after he stopped mentioning his visions. As a result he carried a sense of inadequacy throughout his life, even though he had excelled in high school, college and into the work place, just as his father wanted.

He married Marlene 17 years ago, not because he loved her, but for how she made him feel…like he was king of the mountain. Somewhere within he felt he didn't deserve her love and devotion and deliberately caused friction between them. He would not loosen his grip on his anger for his father. That anger was known and certain. Blaming her for informing others of his dreams was his way of distancing himself from her, before she dropped the other shoe and divorced him. Deep down, he knew it wasn't her.

Secretly he'd tried remedies and potions, which he was told, would curtail his craving for the spirits. He had tried many stratagems: eating a full meal before going out, lining his stomach with olive oil, by just drinking beer, or only drinking after five p.m. He cried, made promises, and even threw in a few "Our Fathers" for good measure, when the craving set in. All to no avail.

Marlene had faith in him. Sometimes it wore a little around the edges, but she never lost it. She seemed to see his virtues even if he didn't. When did things begin to go wrong, he wondered?

Scott graduated with a Ph.D. in Oceanography, joined the Navy, and left the service as a Lieutenant Commander after 12 years. His last duty station was Pearl Harbor, where he quickly snatched up a position at the National Oceanic and Atmospheric Administration upon retiring. Chris was his supervisor.

Smiling, Cuppy was taking in Scott's misery. "Got a big head I'd bet ya."

"Screw you Cuppy," he says, thumping the bar. "Who needs you here? Aren't you supposed to be someplace else…like jacking off in your hole?"

"Already did that this morning. Now I'm looking for some more fun. Wanna play?" Cuppy thrust his thumbs against his cheeks, crossed his eyes, wiggled his fingers, and wagged his tongue in annoyance. He was not at all fond of Scott but placated him for Chris's sake. He thought him self-centered, egotistical, and an arrogant ass, however he did begrudgingly admire his genius and the way he could pull solutions, even for the most difficult of problems, out of thin air.

"I'll get you for this," moaned Scott.

Cuppy threw his hands up in disgust, "Yea? You and who else?"

Chris shot him a stern look.

Cuppy shrugged his shoulders, threw his hands up like a victim in a hold up, and forced an apologetic grin.

With a look that conveyed sympathetic comprehension, Chris asked cautiously, "What's this I hear about you and Marlene?" He knew his friend was not very pleasant when he had a hangover, and was known to bite off a few heads, while nursing a headache. Although he'd covered for him many times, on and off the job during those episodes, he was never given any special breaks or preferential treatment. Perhaps that's why Scott liked him so much. He didn't feel like he was being treated as a subordinate. He displayed an ostentatious austerity, which Chris found annoying, but with which he could live.

Scott possessed clairvoyant gifts beyond anyone's reckoning. One of his unique talents was that he had an innate ability to predict earthquakes and was dubbed "Genius" by his peers. He could accurately guess when the next one would occur before, and more accurately than, any machines or scientists could.

He was valuable to the team, but his drinking was crumbling his career, and many of his peers were avoiding him. When he wanted to go on a binge, he'd pick a fight with his wife for some obscure reason, and then blame her for his pugnacious drunkenness. These binges were becoming more frequent and now Chris wanted to pin block being an enabler. He was tired of being used by Scott and of his refusal to look into how he was contributing to the destruction of his job, marriage and friendships. He'd worn his welcome out everywhere else. Once he possessed qualities of reliability and responsibility that was matched by very few people he had known, but now....

"That guy over there told me you and he got into it over a dream? Is that true? Over a dream?"

For a long moment Scott sat there looking like a discarded marionette. "No, no," he insisted, waving his hand back and forth. "It's my wife. I told her to keep her mouth shut but no, she had to blab to the world."

"What did she tell them Scott?"

"You wouldn't believe me. I don't believe it myself. All I know is it's making me crazy" He shook his head as if to destroy the memory.

"What is it Scott? Come on buddy, I'll listen," Chris pressed on quietly, eager to verify what his version was.

"I heard them talking. I knew she'd been here. She told them about the dreams. She swore she wouldn't tell anyone."

"What about the dreams? Tell me, what about the dreams?" He caught his imagination leaping forward, anticipating what he might say next.

Cuppy and Sky moved closer, their curiosity increasing. They hadn't a clue as to what Chris had eked out of the conversation with the men at the table. Could all three be tied to this thing by an unseen thread? They waited anxiously for Scott's response.

"I don't know," he weakly sobbed, tears rolling down his cheeks. "I can't see whom it is...only hands...sinking...it's drowning," he sobbed. "I can't save it. I can't even swim," he laughed weakly, "but I'm down there. It's so damn real."

Chris's heart raced. An eerie feeling crawled down his spine. It was true...they all had the same dreams. He knew the panic and lack of understanding Scott was feeling. There were a thousand questions with no answers. He understood the despair both Lou and Scott were feeling, as he too had experienced the foreboding, the fear of impending doom. The whole thing unsettled him and he was not sure exactly how to proceed.

"What if I told you weren't the only one to have these dreams? What if I told you both myself and that man over there were having the same dreams?"

For a moment Scott remained silent. "Yeah, right." he retorted. "Then I'd say he's full of shit. He's mocking me I tell you...mocking me. I was gonna get him to shut his big mouth but he backed down," he says in a clear voice that obviously did not care how far it might carry. Spittle flew from his lips. As if protecting himself against an unseen enemy, he crossed his arms tightly across his chest and glared at Lou across the room.

"Scott, look at me," Chris demanded.

His colleague's voice seemed to come from afar. "Here comes the lecture," Scott says sarcastically, rolling his eyes. He was sorry for making that remark because he had known Chris to be fair, just, patient and, his best friend.

Chris leaned into Scott's face. Whiskey reeked from him like fifty-cent cologne. "I said look at me."

Scott straightened his spine and looked Chris Square in the face, to find it was getting redder by the minute. His eyes had narrowed. He

Three Dreams

knew "the look" as he'd seen it many times when he screwed up, and Chris had to call him on the carpet. It was the "I mean business" look and "time to straighten up and fly right" look. "So okay, I'm looking," opening his eyes exaggeratedly.

"Again, what if I tell you others are having the same dreams? What if I could prove it?"

"Yeah sure you can." Scott thought he was being patronized. It would be incredulous that others could be going through this hell.

Chris wondered if the drink wasn't getting to him. He heard stories of drunks with "wet brain" and how they hallucinated. Was Scott on his way?

Chris pressed his arm gently. "I'm not kidding Scott. We've both had them. I see you want proof!"

Scott nodded, pretending to believe him, but inwardly he wasn't sure.

He recounted the same dreams, pausing occasionally to gather his recollections and memories, as he had to with Lou. Scott pantomimed the same reaction. His eyes became large, his mouth fell open and his head was nodding in affirmation the deeper his friend delved into the dreams. His eyes were luminous with relief. Chris deliberately stopped short, at the cabin door. "Is that about it," he concluded.

"Yes, yes, that's it...all of it," he stammered, scarcely able to conceal his amazement." He accepted Chris's knowledge without question. "You couldn't have known unless you'd been there. What the hell is going on? Why is this happening? It can't be a coincidence. And the baby...it can't be real. No child could survive down there. If it did, where's the ship? I haven't heard of any disasters, have you? No, it's impossible...you just heard it somewhere. It's that Marlene...."

Why was it he and Lou could only hear the child crying but weren't allowed entrance, Chris wondered?

"Cuppy and Sky can tell you that I told them about my dreams from the beginning. Several weeks ago, in fact. I thought at first they were a joke, but it's not funny any more. Ask them if you don't believe what I'm saying is true," he insisted.

Scott's expression was skeptical, but he wanted to believe it. He scowled, but complied. He looked to Sky first for validation. If anyone knew Chris, she did.

Yes, she knew Chris. She knew a wonderful, passionate man when she arrived at the Institute more than four years ago. She knew bits and pieces of him disappeared each time the dreams woke him at night. She knew his personality was changing…and she knew he was at war with itself. He tried, unsuccessfully, to pass off the dreams, but she knew they were eating away at him. He had always been in control of his life. Now he was helpless to fix it, and she knew she couldn't.

Sky found very little literature on *congruent* dreams, which only reinforced her negative feelings about them. She felt the dreams weren't random, nor did they appear to have any secretive or masked meaning from a childhood trauma, as research indicated the cause might be. Also, they didn't seem to correlate with any stress on the job, or indicate they had a metaphysical meaning. Therefore, she reasoned, since there was no scientific nor logic to base it on, then they were a fluke. Now that Scott and this other man were experiencing them too, she was more perplexed than ever. What could she say to him, when she didn't know herself?

She tried to recall what little information she eked from the archives, and then she began.

"He told me about it months ago. At first I thought it was a fluke and just laughed it off, but when they continued, the humor soon died. When I saw how they affected Chris, I did some research on my own. I found that maybe it's some kind of ESP or clairvoyance, if someone keeps experiencing the *same* dreams over and over. I read somewhere a woman from Michigan dreamed of a plane crash, twice, and tried to warn the airline, even going so far as to tell them it would be a loose bolt, that would fly into the engine thus, disabling it. No one believed her. When the plane crashed, they too, called it a fluke."

Cuppy interrupted. "There must be something that's beyond all of us as to why the three of you are having the exact same dreams. I don't believe it's a coincidence or a fluke. It seems there's something that going on with you guys, but I can't honestly tell you what, ole buddy."

Ole buddy? Chris raised his eyebrows. Cuppy had never used that term on anyone but him. Could he be feeling compassion for Scott?

"I thought he was nuts when I first heard it…that it was quite an amusing, if not unusual…a dream he'd made up, for laughs," recollected Sky. "I did get a laugh out of it the first couple of times…but now… if he said it happened, I guess it happened. Now you're having them, and that guy over there is too. How do you explain that? Something's happening. Can't be a coincidence. You three seem to be heading for an adventure," she lied.

Leo had been quietly listening to the fascinating details from behind the bar, and was amazed with what he heard. "I can't imagine anything more tragic than knowing a child needed help and we're standing here doing nothing…just talking about it. Let's *do* something. Don't you guys know where it is? I'll help. We'll all help," he says excitedly, hands flailing in the air.

"We don't know the where or the what of this thing, but I think I know someone who can help us get to the bottom of it. I'll give him a call," Chris replied. "Don't worry buddy. We'll find out what's going on.

Abruptly turning, he raised his arm in a good-bye gesture to the three men at the table, who were so intently spinning their own hypothesis among themselves that no one noticed.

Looking at Sky he says, "Let's get out of here. This is my day off. See you guys later." As they left he threw a twenty on the bar.

Roberta M. Alleman

1:30 p.m. June 2

Arriving back at the apartment, they decided to order out after finding their breakfast too cold to eat. Sky called for delivery to appease their hunger. Twenty minutes later the food was delivered. In the kitchen they unwrapped their Rueben sandwiches from the waxed paper, opened a couple of beers, and then carried them to the living room to eat.

They ate in silence for a while.

As Chris stared out the window he remembered the curtains. "What do you think about the curtains? Time to replace them?"

Sky knew exactly what he was up to. Playfully she says, "I think they're okay."

"You've got to be kidding! Look at them!"

"They can go a bit longer...maybe another year." She chuckled to herself.

Chris jumped from his chair and danced over to the sun rotted drapes. He reached up and tugged on the brocade curtain, tinted yellow with age. It tore easily. When he lifted his arm, he wrinkled his nose, as he got a whiff of himself and quickly dropped it.

"You're the decorator here...what you say to some new ones?"

For a moment the look on her face did nothing to encourage him to pursue the matter.

Finally she said, "I *knew* that's what you were getting at. You want *me* to go pick them out, don't you?"

Still unable to detect the note in her voice, he grinned suggestively.

It didn't escape his attention that there was a new hardness in her voice lately.

Today he saw something in her face that put him on guard but resisted the impulse to ask her what was wrong. He didn't want to hear anything heavy on his day off.

He didn't have to ask. She was about to bring it up herself.

"Chris, let me ask you a question," she began slowly, keeping her tone sweetly reasonable.

"Are you proposing?"

"No, nothing like that. Do you think the quality of our relationship has deteriorated lately?" She was fearful; she had mistaken Chris' distance for withdrawal of commitment. She touched him as though her fingers could sense the truth.

It was a loaded question.

"No," he lied. He knew that the quality of their relationship had abruptly changed these past weeks. "Why do you ask?"

Nervously she fussed with the cover page of a magazine. *I can't believe he doesn't see it. Damn you Chris. Why do I have to be the villain?*

She held on to what was left of her patience, and as calmly as she could, she pushed the envelope a little bit further.

"You mean you haven't notice anything...like since this dream thing began? Nothing?"

"Well, maybe a little something, but I've been a bit jittery lately. I guess I've been hard to live with. I know you don't want to have any part of this and are only there for me...and I love you for that."

"You know there's no scientific reasoning for all of this. If there was some medium of proof, some grounds for belief...it's all presumptions, hearsay evidence. I mean, it's beyond belief...really inconceivable that everyone died except this child...don't you think," she asked, exaggerating each word.

Not knowing where she was going with her questions, he offered no response.

"Don't you think you're just chasing your tail? Maybe you all read something into this that's not there. It seems like a lot of fuss over what may turn out to be nothing more than it appears to be, just three people having the same dreams. Coincidence. That's all it is, mere coincidence. Besides, isn't it true that what we experience usually is influenced, arranged, and manifested by our conscious and subconscious minds?"

He shrugged, then spread his hands in a gesture of appeasement and smiled.

"Honey, you may be right. I really don't know. Just hang in there. Let's see where it all goes. I'm not at all sure where the trail will lead either, but I'm willing to give it a few days of my life...and Sky...honey...what if...what if it is true? What if there is a baby that needs rescuing?" His own words made him realize that subconsciously he had already made his decision. "We should know something soon...if not, I'm sure this will burn itself out and I'll be able to get a good night's sleep...then everything will be back to normal."

There was no mistaking the note of finality. She had learned to read his voice. Now he was telling her she had no choice but to follow because he was going to pursue this, no matter where it took him.

It took her a moment to recover. "Oh, I was just wondering." She almost confessed at that point that she thought these dreams were hogwash and wouldn't amount to anything in the long run. Instead, thinking it may be over soon, she resigned herself to run the gamut with him.

She wondered if she had the strength to do it.

Taking another whiff, Chris decided to shower. Heading for the bathroom, his clothes lay where he dropped them as he peeled them off, finishing in the bathroom. He barely noticed himself in the full-length mirror hanging on the door as he stepped into the shower. He backed up to the nozzle head and let the liquid fingers lap against his neck. He sucked in his breath against the hot water, letting the stinging spray massage the tension in his neck, where he stored most of his stress. The ache in his shoulders told him his nerves were stretched to the limits behind this phenomenon, and for once in his life, he didn't have any answers.

While researching for a speech at the Hawaiian State Library on King Street last week he decided to launch his own investigation on the dreams. With the assistance of the knowledgeable research librarian, they pulled every book from the shelves, which might quiet his questioning brain. He climbed the three flights of stairs to the main reading area. Looking for privacy, his eyes skipped over the room, and fell on a reference table that was screened by book stacks. Slipping into an empty chair, he labored over every printed word on the subject, for the next several hours. He poured over journals, magazines, periodicals, documents, computer screens, and other volumes of psychoanalytic texts dedicated to any phenomena on dreams. To no avail. There wasn't much to be found on his particular phenomena.

Although there was much said about others sharing same dreams, there was no written word on congruent dreams. He didn't know any more when he left, than he did when he came in. Disappointed and unable to concentrate, he shelved his own research for another day.

Just then the shower door swung open. "Want company?"

Chris ran his eyes hungrily over her nude body. I'm *dying and going to heaven*, he thought.

Sky slid by him and stepped under the shower. He watched as she lifted her hair to let the water run through. She sensually ran the soap over her body, stopping at the Y of her upper thighs. Although her eyes were closed she knew he was watching her. Without opening them she murmured, "Come here…I'll wash your back."

"Just my back? I need soaping all over," he says teasingly, turning his back to her.

Sky soaped her hands and reached around his hips for him. "Like here?" Her movements began slowly. As he became firm she increased the pace. He could feel her warm breath quicken on his neck, which turned him on even more. Her tongue licked his flesh. He took her hands away. It was too excruciating wonderful. He turned, cradled her face between his palms, and scattered butterfly kisses all over her face as she pressed against the evidence of his desires. *What a lucky, lucky man I am*, he thought. He never loved anyone as he loved her. Breathing softly in her ear he whispered, "Let's go to bed."

In a few moments they were heaving about, her hands digging into his shoulders, his hands moving all over her moist flesh. Both quivered with pleasure. Their passion built. He felt her pull him deeper and deeper into her as she cried in delight. Her eyes were squeezed shut with effort. When she arched her back that was all it took for him to release the throbbing of his member into her. She received his pleasure completely. Arching her body against him, she exploded, and then collapsed.

Chris lay atop of her, too weak to move. His breathing was hard. "I think I'm going to die," he gasped as he finally rolled over, "a wonderful death."

Sky rose, leaned over and kissed him on the stomach, blew a jet of breath over the hairs of his chest, then headed for the bathroom.

"If you give me a minute I'll be ready to go again," he kidded.

"Dreamer!" When she returned a few minutes later Chris was sound asleep with the sheets bunched around his knees. She stared down at him and felt an overwhelming love for this man. He had curled his body in a fetal position. 'My baby,' she thought. Softly she ran her fingers over his skin, admiring its smoothness.

Roberta M. Alleman

    When she had met him, his manner toward her was courteous, but a little aloof. This attracted her, because many men clearly made their wants immediately known. Chris was different. Working side by side she gained respect for him and soon learned he was her peer in many ways. Their personalities accentuated the other, making all the more obvious their individuality. She loved his Roman nose, his dark lashes, the mole on his shoulder, even the healing gash on his on his thigh. She wondered where he had gotten it. As he slept she curled his rich black hair around her fingers. Cupping her body around his, she was very close to sleep. Drifting back and forth across its threshold she wondered, which of them, their child would look like. She blushed slightly and drifted off to sleep. The day dwindled to dusk while they slept to the sound of the gentle rustling of the Walahee tree and the never-ending stirring of the ocean.

9:10 a.m. June 3

Tired of dissembling, Chris called Steve Lawsen, a long time friend from school. He needed to trust someone who may help.

"Hello. Steve? Steve, this is Chris. Yeah Chris. Okay. Doing just fine. Look Steve I need to talk to you. No, it's not that. It's urgent. I need your help.

"No, I don't want to talk about it now. Do you have some time this afternoon?" Pause. "Yes, I know where it is. Six o'clock? That's fine. You *will* be there? Okay, see you then."

They had met at the university, where they had gone for their perspective degrees. Steve was born into money, tons of it. His parents were both prominent Republicans and, although living in the South, had huge money interests in New York and Philadelphia. It was said his father was the richest man in the state.

His father had been a distinguished writer from a long lineage of blue bloods, so it was no surprise when his parents disowned him, when he married the daughter of a Democrat Senator, who was born to a shoemaker and a theater cashier. Resourceful as Steve was, it didn't seem to bother him…he was in love. Although he never worked a day in his life, he immediately attained a position with a local law firm as a law clerk, much to the chagrin of his father. The job kept him busy with research while his wife worked in a nearby bookstore. The marriage lasted eight months before his wife returned home to the guilt her father continuously threw after her, for leaving him and her mother with no emotional support. Although very tempted to do the same, he decided to enroll in college, to show his dad he could make money too. Maybe one day he'd run for office too, he told himself. He selected psychology as his major, which was just as well, Chris reasoned, because he was always nosing into someone else's business. This field could only help him dig in deeper.

They had shared a dorm room, doubled dated, played sports together, and pulled each other out of jams. He joined the Air Force while Chris preferred the Navy. Steve even moved to Hawaii when he learned that Chris had taken a job there. He'd been married three times and thought himself a man about town; however, his wives did not share that fantasy.

A friend once told him that Steve was envious of his abilities, but he wasn't sure that was true. He knew Steve dabbled into the paranormal, ESP, and the like, and was quite learned in the field. Perhaps he could shed some light on what was going on.

Chris was on his way to meet with Steve, when suddenly the windshield filled with the vision of the woman so vivid; it took his breath away. Her face was tear-streaked and her arms were reaching out to him.

"Chris...please help my baby," she pleaded.

As quickly as she had come, she was gone.

It so shocked him that he slammed on the brakes. The car swerved, fishtailed, and slammed to such an abrupt stop that he was forced against the steering wheel. The right wheels came to rest on the sidewalk, knocking over a DO NO PARK sign. A motorist speeding by honked at him.

Shaken, he sat there with his head resting on the steering wheel: his hands still gripping the wheel. He sat there sullenly, feeling like two people. As his breathing began to slow, so did the pounding of his heart. How did she know his name? His hands trembled as he loosened his grasp on the wheel. My God, who was that? Cripes, what's happening to me, he wondered. Where is this ever going to end?

She was the woman from his dreams. Who the hell was she and where did she come from, he wondered. Why was she intruding in his life? Or was she really there at all? So far the answers eluded him.

Still trembling, he put the car in gear, scanned the street for traffic and then eased the car back off the curb. He noticed a scraping sound he hadn't heard before, and decided it must be the fender rubbing against the tire.

4:50 p.m. June 3

Chris was only just beginning to calm down when he reached the *Coral Reef. He* found Steve already there, beckoning him over to a corner table. Leaving a client just twenty minutes earlier, he was dressed in a dark suit embellished with a red tie and handkerchief. His five foot eleven frame still held its youthful and boyish look although he was approaching forty. He had developed a reputation as a playboy, a notion he did not try to discourage. His hairline had receded somewhat, but was barely noticeable with his curly hair. He had the kind of hair women would kill for, but that was the *only* thing Steve never seemed to appreciate about himself. He had always found it most annoying.

A smile bloomed on his face. "I hope this is okay. It offers privacy," he says, extending his hand.

"It's fine," Chris replied, shaking his hand firmly. You're early."

"Finished sooner than I expected. What are you drinking?"

"Scotch rocks."

"Waiter," he called, waving his finger in the air, "two Scotch rocks please."

Seeing the anguish in Chris's eyes, he asked what was bothering him.

"I'm not sure where to begin Steve. It's all so crazy. I have to talk to someone who'll give me some intelligent feedback and not a lot of theories."

"The truth shall set you free," Steve chimed.

The waiter arrived with their drinks and spilled their overflowing contents onto the table. "Sorry Sir," he mumbled.

"No biggy. Just keep an eye on us, and when we're empty, bring us another."

The waiter awkwardly dabbed at the moisture, and then withdrew.

Chris stared at his drink, not sure where to begin. He thought of what Steve had said. *Yes*, he thought, *maybe I can purge myself of this if I dump it. Maybe the truth will set me free…Steve's impartial.*

With as much steadiness as he could muster, he began.

"Well, it all started about six weeks ago…" He went on for the next hour recounting his dreams, the visions, Scott, Lou and everything else that may have any connection that might tie at all together.

Steve had settled his well-fleshed body into his chair. He listened quietly, occasionally nodding his head, while sipping his drinks.

"I just don't know what to make of it," Chris ended, scrutinizing Steve for signs of understanding.

Wordlessly, emotions masked, Steve placed his hand on Chris's arm. He stared at him for a few moments, as if his friend had lost it. The pause lengthened.

Steve had a sudden vision of the absurdity of at all. He smiled, as if he was about to play a trump card. "You're kidding! Right? It's some kind of a joke, right," he laughed, looking about the room as if expecting to see *Candid Camera* cameras lurking behind potted palms.

Chris felt the blood leave his face. Hope dried up in his chest like an autumn leaf thrown into a flame. His mouth went dry. His jaws tightened. He gripped the arms of the chair and pushed forward, preparing to flee.

Chris's head shot toward Steve. "**God damn it!**" His tone was sarcastic. Although his first impulse was to leave, he thought better of it. *Of course he thinks I'm kidding...it's crazy. Who, in their right mind would believe it?*

"Do you realize the hell I... we, have been going through day and night, trying to figure out the answers ourselves," he asked, taking a deep breath. "Don't you think that before we discovered what we had in common that we each thought we were losing it? If there's **any** comfort in this, it's that I now know I'm not as crazy as I thought I was," he barked, shaking his head as if to rid himself of the idea.

For a moment Steve was shocked by Chris's anger. Then he wondered why he was surprised. He could see this thing was really bothering him. A flicker of something crossed his face. Realizing he had made a mistake in judgment he quickly said, "I'm sorry, I'm sorry. I thought you were pulling my leg. Your imagination...or what I thought was your imagination stunned me. I..."

Chris silenced him with a wave of his hand. "Just listen for a minute will you?"

Steve settled back in his chair and smiled apologetically. He extended his hand, then waved it in front of him, as if giving him the floor.

Three Dreams

The agony of what he felt was almost impossible to put into words. "I know it's weird. No one has to tell me that, but I didn't think you'd find it so funny. *You're* the so-called expert in the paranormal. *You're* supposed to know about this stuff. Tell me Steve, have you ever heard of anything remotely like this," he asked softly, feeling emotionally bankrupt.

Steve tossed off the last of the scotch in his glass. Catching the bartender's eye, he held the empty glass up, pointed to it, and yelled, "Please. Two more."

"Look, we can't get anywhere by getting drunk."

Ignoring him Steve began, "You three men seem to have knowledge of things far beyond your area of perception; second sight, as it were. It seems you're tuned into something that is yet to happen…the sinking of the ship perhaps. Maybe the child or the ship is a *symbol* of something else. Maybe it's precognition, which is the power to see into the future…to know about an event before it happens. What's the cause, and where it comes from, has had scientists pacing the floor and scratching their heads for years. It's hard to understand. No one knows how anyone can predict what's going to happen in the future."

Chris came to that conclusion when he had done his own research.

"There are some people who have ESP. The clinical term is **"extra sense-ory**," which gives people the powers of perception of external objects to events not directly accessible to any of the other sense organs. The operative word is *extra*. It seems you three are experiencing this phenomenon, but why all three are having them simultaneously, is a new on me. Usually people dream of the same event but from different angles…but not you guys.

"How can we find out what's going on?"

"We can't, yet. Several people predicted the sinking of the Titanic days, weeks, before it happened," Steve answered, motioning for the check. "I'll have to do some research. I, uh, I've got some friends. I'll talk to my colleagues, so give it a few days. Waiting is the name of the game now."

The waiter arrived with the check, which Steve quickly paid with his Master Card, leaving the waiter a ten-dollar cash tip on the table.

As they stood to leave, they clasped hands firmly and moved toward the door.

"Whaaagh. Whaaagh."

Chris's hair stood up on the back of his neck. He quickly glanced about the room seeking the origin of the cry. He focused on a mother attempting to quiet her child, while entering the connected dining room. For a few brief moments, the reality of the situation overtook him and he realized he was no longer in control. He was back at the ship, adrenaline pumping, reaching for the crying infant, but unable to reach it. Sweat beaded on his upper lip. His eyes flashed about as he gripped the bar rail to steady himself.

Witnessing his reaction, Steve was concerned Chris was going over the edge. He put his arm around his shoulder in an attempt to calm him, and then ordered him a drink. Chris waved it off. Although his entire body still trembled, he managed to compose himself enough within a few minutes, to make it to his car. If Steve didn't believe him before, he wondered now. He knew he had to get his friend some help.

Steve couldn't believe his reaction, just from a child's cries. Several people who were waiting to be seated, were staring at him, and whispered among themselves. Embarrassed, he fled to his car with Steve in hot pursuit.

Pulling on the car door handle, it opened easily. Chris felt relieved he'd left the car unlocked and swiftly slid into the seat. Shaking, he grasped the steering wheel tightly in an attempt to slow his tremors. His heart pounded.

Steve stood there, speechless, watching his friend hunched over in the front seat like an old woman in prayer.

"I told you Steve, this is no joke. I've gotta go. Call me. I've gotta go," he said, as he slammed the door shut and sped off, tires squealing.

A few minutes later the jack hammering in his chest had slowed to a thump-thump. His hands had almost stopped trembling. Without even pausing at the stop sign, Chris yanked hard on the wheel; turned left and entered North Street. Stomping on the accelerator, he sped toward home in the deepening twilight. Where one community ended and the next began was now indistinguishable. The route home was automatic.

1.30 p.m. June 4

Steve finally called, inviting the three men over to his office. He was annoyingly brief in his reasons, only to say, to be there at five that evening, and that the three must come together. One or two absolutely would not do. He left the details up to Chris.

The cloaked excitement in Steve's voice gave Chris the eerie feeling he was hiding an ace up his sleeve. He couldn't help but wonder what he had discovered. It was going to be difficult to wait until five to find out.

They arrived a few minutes early, apprehensive of what information Steve had to offer. Entering the burgundy carpeted foyer; they found the only elevator emptying its passengers. The elevator bounced to a stop at the fifth floor, leaving Scott's stomach high in his throat. The corridor was empty, save for a large Rubber Tree plant. Half way down they found Steve's office.

After a perfunctory screening by the receptionist, who sat dutifully stationed at her desk, they sat and waited. Lou thought she bore a strong likeness to Flo of TV's *Mel's Café*.

Instantly Scott didn't trust her. As she questioned him, his ears focused while his peripheral vision scanned the room…looking for what, he did not know.

While they waited their eyes traveled with curiosity about the room. The waiting room looked typical of one where the head honcho was making big bucks. It smelled of old wood but was tastefully furnished. The walls were lined with framed photographs of Hawaii's most prominent citizens, and, of course, Steve was in each of them. He had always appreciated successful people regardless of their qualities, which also reflected in his reading material. Magazines were placed strategically on the mahogany table. Chris knew it was meant to intimidate or to impress. They held such names as *Newsweek, The Robb Report, Dupont Registry of Fine Homes* and polished newspapers like *The European Sunday Times of London* and the *Wall Street Journal*. Travelogues informed the reader of exotic far away places and points of interest for the elite. *La de dah*, thought Chris. *Who's he trying to kid? I bet he never turned a page on any one of these things. He wouldn't have been caught dead within thirty feet of this stuff in school. He'd be lucky if he opened a comic book.*

As they waited Lou picked up a magazine and thumbed through it idly while Scott slouched in his chair and tried to doze.

Ten minutes later Steve appeared in his office doorway. He wore a gray suite, a charcoal tie, which was framed by a beige shirt, and a matching handkerchief. He beckoned them in, closing the door gently behind them as if it were a fragile friend.

His office was tastily furnished in the same mahogany theme as the outer office. The organized clutter on his desk gave Chris the impression it was there for effect. A muffled humming noise percolated from the next room. He motioned for them to be seated in the chairs, which were angled to the left of the room. Seating himself behind the desk, he placed his elbows on a stack of papers and folded his hands before him as if he were going to pray. Leaning forward in his chair until his chin was directly over his hands, he stared, making eye contact with each.

The anxious men exchanged quizzical glances at each other, then back at him.

Chris couldn't read any expression behind those penetrating eyes.

Annoyed, after a few moments of glaring at each other, anger found its way into Scott's voice. "Did we come here for a staring contest or are we supposed to read each other's minds?"

"I was wondering to what lengths you three are willing to go through to get to the bottom of this."

"What's that supposed to mean?" Angry, Lou jumped so suddenly from his chair that he almost knocked it over. "We're here, ain't we? Spit it out mate." He wondered if Steve was stupid, or just insensitive to what they were experiencing. *Probably just stupid*, he thought.

Scott too, was becoming impatient. His face flushed with anger. He was never crazy about Steve and considered him a self-centered S.O.B. Why was he playing a cat and mouse game? "For Christ's sake get to the point. We'll judge the rest for ourselves. If not, I'm out of here."

He'd be more than glad to fill his hours with other matters.

Smiling, he said, "I want you to hear me out before you say anything. Agreed?" His smile was devoid of warmth.

Lou sagged into his chair, as if defeated, and eyed him suspiciously. He was tired of these unsolicited circumstances that have almost wrecked his life…awake and asleep. He wanted his life back, and he wanted more than anything to vanish into a dreamless sleep. "Out with it man," he says impatiently. Tension crackled in the air around them.

Chris wanted to tell him to get on with it too, but after so many years of knowing Steve, he knew he'd spit it out when he was good and ready. He was an expert in setting the stage. He suspected he wouldn't go through all this unless he had a salutary finale.

Well," he began slowly, "I've consulted with my colleagues. They're most intrigued, to say the least. We spent many hours on the Internet and phones and we think we've come up with something," he said as he stood. "Please, come this way. I want you to meet one of the most distinguished illustrious scientists in the field of the paranormal, alive today. She really knows her stuff. As luck has it she's in town for her daughter's wedding. Her sister-in-law and my sister-in-law are related by marriage. Follow me."

What a jerk thought Lou. *What the hell is he talking about? We don't need scientists; we need psychiatrists, if you ask me.*

Entering the adjacent room they let their eyes circuit the room. All eyes took in the same picture. A handful of equipment with electrodes hanging from them, like octopus arms and other paraphernalia was situated throughout. The walls were an offensive yellow with bare sash windows, save for a few dust webs. An uncommonly grayish, threadbare carpet, which made a crunching sound, like walking in snow, lay sprawled out like some slain science fiction monster.

Three sets of eyes shifted to the three gurneys in the middle of the room.

"Damn, they're gonna open us up," said Lou, his mind racing ahead of the consequences. "I'm not going that far."

"Relax, no one is having surgery," responded a voice from behind. All eyes turned toward the voice. Entering the room, carrying an armful of books and files, was a woman about 55, who resembled Ethel Mertz of the *Lucy Show*. Her snow-white hair, tied back in a bun, had wisps of hair that fluttered like gossamer wings when she moved. She was thick, but not fat and wore an open lab coat with several pens jutting from the breast pocket. Ink stains surrounded the distended hole, which was becoming frayed with many years of use.

As if reading their mind she says, "It's my lucky coat."

Two frock-coated men of Asian descent followed her, supporting what appeared to be, two microwave ovens. "And we're not going to cook you either. We merely want to conduct some experiments that will help us better understand this phenomena.

My name is Doctor Malik from the Devlin Institute." After placing the files on a nearby table she turned and shook hands warmly with each of them, pausing for a moment to scrutinize each, before moving on to the next. "Steve's story has us intrigued."

Pointing to several TV screens supported on the walls she continued, "We are connected by closed circuit TV to several scientists from four institutes, who are monitoring and assisting in our research. They're equally interested in the results."

"What do you mean...research? Don't you know what you're doing," Lou asked warily.

"I know you're curious about the connection the three of you might have to these dreams. We too, want to know. However, shared dreams are not that uncommon. We've been researching these phenomena for decades. People have been predicting future events, through dreams, as long as man has been around. Usually these dreams are seen from different angles, much like sitting in different seats at a football game. But your dreams seem to be *exactly* alike...just as if you were sitting in the same seat. That's what we want to know more about...why. We've been experimenting with a recent discovery that may give us some insight to that question.

"Please gentlemen, select a gurney. I'll explain everything as I go along. Your bodies will not be intruded upon. We will be putting you to sleep simultaneously. It's during the rapid eye movement, REM sleep, as it's called, that we do most of our dreaming and, where we're more likely to get a dream report. We can visually see when you're in this stage and that's when we'll conduct our tests. Your sleep will be monitored, measured, charted, evaluated and studied. Later, my colleagues and I will interpret the data, and perhaps, come up with some answers for you.

"Are you ready," she asked as if she already knew they would agree.

They exchanged glances, warily selected a gurney, and lay down. The two anonymous assistants busied themselves connecting them to wires and gadgets, which would monitor their breathing, pulse, brain impulses, heart rate, and other statistics that would later be interpreted by the observers

Lou was clearly an unwilling participant. He had a longstanding fear of needles and asked if they had a pill he could take, instead.

"Afraid of needles," asked the assistant, with an exaggerated smile.

"I had a better time in intensive care," he says, protectively pulling his arms tightly to his chest.

"All you'll feel is a tiny prick, I promise you. We must do this quickly...you must reach the REM stage simultaneously. Now give me your arm," anonymous number one quipped. Reluctantly, Lou extended his arm, pulled up his sleeve and offered his forearm to the hypo.

As he went under he murmured, "Say, I didn't feel a th...."

Roberta M. Alleman

7:28 p.m. June 4

When the tests were complete, Dr Malik asked them to meet with her in the outer office.

Fifteen minutes later she emerged alone, looking puzzled.

"It seems you gentlemen are somehow connected as one mind while you're asleep. It's quite an unusual case, I must say." She reached up and placed her hand on the back of her neck. "Actually we have never encountered anything like this before, so we're learning with you. As you may know, we usually go through four stages of sleep. The first is where we start to lose consciousness, or are, in essence, 'falling asleep.' Then there's stage two where we stay for about 10 to 20 minutes. It's where our brains begin to synchronize activity. This means the brain begins to work together, with no distractions. While awake all parts of our brains work separately. For instance, we are driving down the street: we watch for pedestrians, we light up a cigarette, we're thinking about picking up our dry cleaning, we're distracted by a headache and a number of other activities. In stage two all the parts pull together with no distractions. In stage three, the brain is highly synchronized, or in deep sleep, but we begin to climb out of this stage, for unknown reasons, and go back to stage two. In the fourth stage we are propelled into dream sleep, or REM sleep. These four stages repeat themselves every ninety minutes...maybe four or five times a night, depending on how long you sleep. Well you don't. You wake up after *each* four-stage cycle, terrified, remembering every vivid detail. That's why you remember your dreams so clearly. Do this over and over again, night after night, it's no wonder you think you're crazy."

"Why *do* we dream, doc," Lou asks.

"No one knows exactly what function it performs for the mind. Some think we dream to resolve problems...find answers. Others think they're telegrams sent from ourselves, to ourselves, telling us to do, or not to do something. Then again, are they prophecies? Do they stimulate the creative mind? Or, are they there to keep us sane? No one really knows. The archives are full of people who've dreamed about a coming event but not *exactly*. Four years ago six people dreamed of an overloaded ferry capsizing and saw people trapped and drowning. Each thought it was a nightmare. Three reported their part of the dream to their families. Two wrote it down. The last attempted to contact the company she thought owned the ferry, only to be dismissed as a crank. She had 'watched' 56 people drown, in her dream, and fought to dissuade fate. She felt she'd be responsible for their deaths if she didn't try to stop it. Needless to say they were all affected when the tragedy came to pass, but she took the news the hardest. This brave woman thought, if she'd been more persistent, then *maybe* it wouldn't have happened. The difference? Each shared a *part* of the story in their dream. You share the *same congruent* experiences, and yours is more insistently delivered.

Lou nodded, and Scott said softly, "I couldn't handle something like that. "I can't even handle one baby drowning let alone a boat full. How can we know if this is true? Isn't it a bit preposterous? I mean, a ship sinking and there's one survivor? Come on…what's the chance of that happening? I mean, really…." His disbelief was evident in his words. "And what about us? Why were *we* 'chosen'?" He shook his head and gave the doctor an exasperated look.

"How can we stop the dreams doc? How will we know, which ship, where, when…how can we know? Will it be today or has it already happened? How will we get the baby out of there—-if there is a baby? They don't have equipment for stuff like that. It's too bizarre," said Scott.

From the corner of his eye Chris saw Lou remove a small notebook from his breast pocket and jotted down some notes.

"Your brains, being human, are trying to come to terms by organizing and integrating ambiguous experiences into coherent meaning, however, I think we'll have more answers when the results come in. God works in mysterious ways gentlemen. He'll guide us…of that I'm sure," Doctor Malik says softly. "You may not see it yet, but don't lose sight of it."

Lou cocked his head and gave her a salute.

She returned the salute with a grin. "You men go get something to eat and come back in a few hours. Now let me get to work.

9:27 p.m. June 4

Doctor Malik was awaiting them when they returned. Their attention was riveted on her while she studied the back of her hand for a minute.

Steve sat off to the side but gave no indication if he knew anything.

Nervous glances were exchanged.

She began slowly. "It seems you three are connected as one mind when asleep. We already knew this. We think you're experiencing some sort of clairvoyance, or premonition, but we've been unable to determine what, or why there is a common thread between you. Research is full of shared dream experiences, as we discussed, but not like this. The difference? Each person experiences a part of the story much like each chapter of a book. You share the whole book"

Lou gave a deep sigh and said, "Look doc, this is a problem. Is this real or imagined? Is there a child alive somewhere? How can we know if these dreams aren't just a phase, a fluke...and if it is...how do we stop them? I'm sure I'm speaking for the others when I say we're tired. We just want a peaceful night sleep. Can you help us?"

"We'll continue analyzing the data we've gathered. Our colleagues are working on that information at this very moment. This is a new slant on something we thought we knew everything about. There's much we have to learn about the brain. Perhaps a few bad dreams aren't too high a price to pay to save a life."

Chris thought she knew more than she was revealing.

Dr Malik turned and looked at Chris full in the face. "You haven't said much Mr. Healey. Is there something you need to tell me...us?"

Chris's stomach sank. How could she have known he had been holding something back?

"Chris has something he wants to share with you," she said, as she crossed her arms and leaned against the desk. "The door, Mr. Healy?"

She was giving him the floor.

He smiled to hide his dismay.

"Well...yes...ah...well...." He struggled for words, wondering why he hadn't told anyone but Sky and Cuppy that he had gone through the door and had indeed, seen the child.

Three Dreams

With an engaging smile, Steve, who had been sitting quietly in the corner, nodded his head in affirmation.

How could she know, he wondered. *Did Steve tell her? He must have.*

Chris walked to the window and looked out. He stood there for a few moments, trying to gather the right words. Turning, he gave a soft snort of laughter of embarrassment. He saw that no one shared his humor. Taking a deep breath, then began. He disclosed what he had seen inside the cabin…the hands, the woman…the baby, and how he was jerked out of the dream, just as he reached for the child.

"Well I'll be a S.O.B. What's the secret? And better yet, how come you got in and we didn't," Lou asked.

"Yeah! What about that," asks Scott, rising from his seat? "How come you, and not us? What makes you so special?"

"I don't know why I didn't tell you. Maybe it's because I couldn't believe it myself. I thought I was nuts until I heard you two were dreaming the same dreams. You were having your own problems. I didn't want to add to them by having you analyze why I got in and you two didn't. Tell me, weren't you checking your own sanity then? Didn't you think this whole thing was too fantastic to be real? Well, I certainly did"

No one responded.

Pushing herself away from the desk, Dr Malik walked over and put her arms around Lou and Scott. "It doesn't matter why, gentlemen. The fact is, there is, or will be, a real live child down there. You three are destined to play a part in this. It's Chris's fate, we believe, to carry the child from the ocean bottom. Why? We don't know. We think that's the reason he was allowed inside. Something, or someone, has chosen him. How and when this will occur, we don't know that either, but you can bet it will indeed happen, and soon. We'll have to wait and see. Sometimes a message is so strong that it repeats itself until it's received," she said, smiling. Her eyes fixed on Chris. "Rarely are we contacted by someone we don't know or we are not related to in this life. Some things do survive physical death."

Chris felt she was trying to tell him to think harder, and to search his memory, and that perhaps he did know the woman with red hair.

"We'll be in constant contact with collaborating institutes, so go home and wait to hear from us. If anything, anything, unusual happens, calls us immediately." Handing each a card she added, "this number will get you right through to one of us. Don't wait. Call us immediately; no matter how insignificant you think it is. Call us right away."

She shook hands with them, turned abruptly on her heels and left the room. Her two assistants folded into the doorway behind her and quietly closed the door behind them.

Dr Malik and her colleagues would search for the key, the missing link that would, hopefully, tie everything together. Was there a test she didn't give? A result she might have missed? A rock she had not overturned? She, and her assistants, would be driven to find out what tied these men and their dreams together.

Steve, who had been uncharacteristically silent throughout, rose from his chair in the corner of the room.

"Well buddy, I guess that's it for now. I hope I did you a good deed by getting these folks involved. They really know their stuff...cream of the crop in their field...well respected." He sounded as if were trying to sell these people to them. "So just wait for their call. I'm sure they'll find something...some good news. Smiling, he vigiously shook their hands with a sweaty grasp as they filed through the door.

When he returned from escorting them to the elevator, he locked the door, and then collapsed a heap in the leather armchair. *Christ*, he thought, *what have I gotten myself, and them, into*? He felt the muscles in his stomach tense.

"Eleanor...Eleanor, he yelled to his secretary. "You can go home now. Take the morning off. Not much happening anyway. Okay?"

"All right," her voice returned from the outer office. "See ya tomorrow afternoon. If ya need me, just call. Good night Mr. Lawson."

Reflecting on what he had heard these past days, he wondered if all this could really be true. Covertly, in the beginning, he was humoring Chris, attributing the dreams to stress, but now.... Could what the doctors said be true? "Well, I'm not going to worry about it now," he says aloud to an invisible audience. Reaching into his jacket pocket, he pulled out a Cuban cigar. Unfortunately, or fortunately, he could not find a light.

Without so much as a twinge of guilt Steve's Secretary Eleanor, picked up the phone and called the *Honolulu Gazette.* It was too good a story *not* to tell. When she told them about her 'scoop' they were more than eager to talk to her.

Roberta M. Alleman

11:49 p.m. June 5

During the drive home Scott was unusually quiet while Lou and Chris discussed Lou's life story and exchanged ideas about his inventions.

His mind bled back in time. Something was coming over him but he couldn't put his finger on what it was. Something deep within was encouraging him to stop drinking and it scared him. Its onset began with the dreams. Previous he drank out of the despair within and drank to anesthetize it. He was beginning to realize he had become a prisoner of his own intellect, alive only from the neck up.

His innate ability to predict earthquakes, he deluded himself, was because he was "cursed." Using alcohol as a crutch for his sense of inadequacy only begot guilt, and depression. Most of all he feared for the thousands of lives that could be lost, if his predictions ever proved wrong. He was a regular and devoted drinker and drank to crowd out those thoughts. He attributed his 'curse/gift' to the inherent ability to 'feel' shock waves in advance of the catastrophe. It was like he had his finger on the pulse of the earth. People theorized he was even more sensitive than any seismograph. If he drank himself into oblivion he wouldn't have to feel responsible, if people died because he did, or did not predict an oncoming disaster. If he stayed drunk, and turned out to be wrong, then he wouldn't be blamed. Would he?

His predictions were called superhuman. Colleagues pleaded with him to tell them the secret in his accuracy. He was asked over and over again, 'How do you do it?' He had asked himself the same question a million times. He truly didn't know.

As they neared home, he scrambled to remember all the things he'd said to Marlene, while under the influence, these past days. Too many mornings he had awakened, wondering what happened the night before and what terrible things he may erupt on his faithful wife.

Unbeknown to anyone, Scott was really trying to clean up his act. He knew his behavior had driven a wedge between himself and his wife, who, he thought, was one hair away from leaving him. He knew he only stayed with her because his feelings of isolation and aloneness were more bearable when she was near. His bitterness spewed out upon her like an uncorked champagne bottle that had been shaken

Three Dreams

vigorously before opening. She always sat there quietly and listened, with tears streaming down her cheeks. Always, he'd later reproach himself. Always he'd cry and say he was sorry. Always, she'd forgive him. The circle went around and around. He didn't know his drinking and self-imposed solitary confinement held her prisoner as well. He had little faith in his ability to hold on to her. He was sure that one day she'd come to him, tell him she'd had enough, and then leave him. He couldn't bear the thought of it.

His eyes grew misty with the past.

"Poor Marlene," he says softly. The throbbing between his ears made him wince. *I bet she thinks I'm out drinking tonight. Know what? I don't want to.*

"What'd you say," asked Lou.

"Nothing. Just talking to myself. Something I forgot to do."

"We're nearly there," Chris says over his shoulder, "better get it together."

Where had his pride, dignity and self-respect gone? He was a puzzle box full of charades. Throughout the years one box after another had been opened and discarded until finally the last one, when opened, was empty. He had insolated himself against the penalties of his own folly. Drinking was a ruinous undertaking, and he knew it. Only Marlene knew of his gift, (although Chris strongly suspected it for years. Too many coincidences.) and encouraged him to use it help people. She knew Scott's parents and relatives had done their job well, in convincing him he'd come from the seed of the devil. As a result, the 'gift' was hidden away, lest others see him as 'doin' the devil's work.' Fear of discovery and self-denial coexisted side by side throughout his life. He thought he felt trapped by the choices he made.

Scott searched his mind. Whatever happened to that carefree guy who had put himself through college while working all sorts of odd jobs? Yeah, what happened to me? He smiled when he thought of some of the positions he once held while putting himself through school: painter, limo driver, pizza delivery, DJ, tutor, sales clerk and others he couldn't recall. Much of his remaining earnings were spent trying to please his father. Now his father was gone into everlasting silence. He knew his father was emotionally bankrupt and wondered if his grandfather had anything to do with it. Something must have happened to make him into the rigid man he had become.

Roberta M. Alleman

A voice whispered in his ear. *"Dwell upon the gift, which has been given to you from the Father—the gift of the realized Presence within you. He has appointed you men for this task and you will bring light to those who need renewed hope."*

Startled. he snapped his head around, just as if he had been hit hard across the face, to see where the voice was coming from. It sounded close enough to have come from someone who might be sitting next to him, but there was no one there. Her voice was soft, angelic. He began to tremble. My God, what's happening to me, he wondered. Now I'm hearing voices. He felt as though another piece of reality had just detached itself and slipped away.

"You guys hear that?" he says.

"Hear what," says Chris.

He wondered if he should tell them of what he just heard, but thought better of it. They wouldn't believe it anyway.

"Oh nothing. Just thought I heard something."

Just then, Chris pulled into the driveway of Scott's small bungalow. Its yellow paint had faded from too many years in the hot sun without care. Curling remnants of green paint clung to sun baked shutters, refusing to give up their claim in the home.

The yellowish-brown yard screamed for moisture and a manicure. A grid of tangled vines, with overgrown tendrils, laid strewn across the arid sidewalk in their desperate search for water. The place looked, overall, like it was just short of being condemned, even in the dark. It was a tumbledown house—-not a home.

Now, the porch light was the only warmth this house had to offer.

Marlene emerged from the front door, slamming the screen behind her. She looked tired, and with her graying hair, appeared older than her 43 years. Chris's heart went out to her. He knew she was going through hell with Scott, because he knew he was. She had telephoned him late several times, frantic with worry, when Scott hadn't come home. Chris wondered why she stayed with a drunk, who treated her more like a servant than a wife. She deserved better.

Marlene, the only child born to Elizabeth and Tom Turner, was raised in Springville, IL; a small town near the City College Scott attended for two years. She and Scott met when he stopped in the *Hamburger Heaven* where she was working. When she first came to take his order he was immediately taken by her, probably because she made a fuss over him. After that he made a habit of coming in as often as his budget would allow. Many times she would playfully call him Frank Sinatra in earlier years, but when his hair began to thin and he began to look gaunt, the comparison waned.

It wasn't long before he learned her parents had owned the café, and that it was failing. He wasn't aware at the time, but the few customers who did come in, were treated like kings, in hopes they would return. It wasn't until they changed from selling burgers and switched to making pizza that it began to thrive.

He found Marlene was bright and funny so it wasn't long before they were dating. They married two years later. Before he went back to the university for his last semester, he left her with her parents. She knew he didn't love her, but felt he would come to—-one day. Until then she felt she had enough love for both of them. She'd wait. She was good at waiting.

She raised her soft eyes to his. "How'd it go honey?" One hand clutched the other to her chest. Her heart jumped for joy. She instantly knew he hadn't been drinking.

"Okay, I guess. Don't know any more than I did before. Did have a good nap though." Smiling, he cracked his knuckles to relieve the tension he felt rising from within.

Every one chuckled. Suddenly, however, all amusement was gone.

There was an uncomfortable silence for a few moments.

"This here's Lou...the other man."

They forced another laugh.

Marlene looked attentively at Lou, as if trying to see deep within his mind, to discover why they shared dreams with her husband, when she couldn't.

"Pleased to meet you Lou. Would you gentlemen like to come in for coffee...had some ready for Lou?" She was sorry she put it that way but now it was too late. "He has some with dinner," she quickly added, wringing her hands.

Understanding her discomfort Chris says, "I know how much of that stuff he drinks at the office...bet the pot's on all the time here." He saw a look of relief came over her face and she secretly nodded to him in gratitude. "Wish we had some of your good coffee at the office Marlene. Whoever makes ours makes it like liquid tar. That stuff is terrible," he says, making a face.

Feeling awkward Lou says, "well, I've got to get going, but thanks anyway. Catch up with ya later Scott—-Ma'am."

As they drove to the docks the two men fell into deep conversation as if they had known each other for years. Chris found himself driving slower as he became more intrigued by Lou. Traffic was light at that hour.

He surmised, by the conversation, that Lou had been pretty much a loner most of his life, only socializing with a few select friends. His childhood curiosity as to how mechanical things worked, led him first to small repairs, then to inventing things out of discarded appliances and old auto parts. He received his first patent for his invention at the age of sixteen and has owned several others since. At age 28 he received his Ph.D. in Mechanical Engineering, but left the field after a few years, for whatever reason, Chris wasn't privy to.

Chris became intrigued when Lou told him that he had been working on an invention for the past three years. It would enable oceanographers and other scientists to capture live specimens from deep in the ocean, under pressure, and bring them to the surface unharmed. The uniqueness about his recent invention was that it was remotely controlled, and could be operated without hoses and the cumbersome undersea robotic arms of diving saucers, that are currently used. With its ability to withstand intense pressure, one could go the depths of the ocean and could safely control the apparatus from quite a distance without disrupting sea life, while maintaining its precious cargo.

The invention would be worth its weight in gold. Chris had contemplated offering seed money to him, but thought better of it, after he remembered Lou saying he had 'quite a bankroll socked away' from the proceeds of his inventions.

Making a living with the sea was Lou's childhood dreams come true, but Chris thought him to be a much deeper, complex person than a simple deck hand.

Little did he know.

6:30 a.m. June 5

Chris received a call from Dr. Malik inviting the men back to Steve's office that morning at 9:30.

They arrived on time, disquieted by what they thought they might hear.

Steve appeared from his office as they entered, and ushered them immediately into where Dr Malik and two other men were already seated. They recognized anonymous assistant number one, but not the other.

Chris searched their faces for clues, which were not forthcoming.

"They've been up all night," Steve began. "Doctors Isu and Malik, along with their associates...."

Abruptly, a small, slightly bent man rose and held up his hand, commanding silence. He bowed in a stiff dignified way, and then paced up and down with his arms banded around him. The silence hung, like a cold fog in the night. Everyone waited in anticipation.

"I'm Doctor Isu," he finally says while extending his hand, "a colleague of Dr Malik."

His sharp eyes of eighty years took in everything at a glance. He wore a tweed jacket that was dated in the 60's, which had a frayed tear in the sleeve and another one on the left pocket. The right pocket was jammed with pieces of paper, notebooks, pens, pencils and a Tootsie Pop. His steel rimmed glasses were too large for his practically unlined oriental face and rested on his mid cheek. Soft wavy gray hair (rare with Asians) peppered with silver threads cascaded over his brow making his face look even smaller. Small wisps of curls had wrapped themselves around his glass stems. He wore a simple loop earring, which he toyed with when in deep thought. His once brisk walk had slowed to a hesitating limp due to a fall from a horse while in the Chinese Navy.

Dr. Isu was not afraid of having, and asserting, his own opinions. Beneath his soft demeanor, gentle manners and agreeability, he was tough and iron willed. With everything he said he sounded as if he knew exactly what he was talking about and expected everyone to support him in his opinions and projects, without question. Most did, and those who didn't, weren't around very long. He was revered, not only in his field, but also in others. He had participated in thousands of experiments throughout the years, all over the world. Were it not for his keen fascination with the paranormal he might have lived out his life as an Agricultural Chemist, which, was his second love.

"We've gone over the data and this much we are sure of. The three of you *are* experiencing the same dreams. The EEGs, which measured the activity of neurons in your brains, were measured before, during and after your REM sleep. The waveforms indicated each of you responded as the others did, with no deviation, except for you, Mr. Healey. Yours continued longer than the others did. "Unusual…most unusual," he said, almost to himself, not stopping to ask why. "During your Rapid Eye movement, as you were told previously, you were experiencing the same events simultaneously."

"So…other than that you didn't find anything…huh," Scott interrupted, looking down at his lap, disappointed.

"On the contrary, this is a Para psychological event. A one of a kind you might say." Dr Isu began slowly as if he were choosing each thought carefully. He smiled when he made eye contact with them. Scanning the papers on Steve's desk he continued, "These dreams are penetrating the heavy barrier of the psyche and you are attempting to ward them off. Dr Elmer Green and his wife of the Menninger Foundation once wrote, and I quote, *"ESP implies that the nature of the mind, even if not logically explainable, includes at least one additional dimension of substance beyond the bounds of the presently defined three dimensional control nervous system."*

"We have defenses, which protects us against what we think doesn't belong in our mind, as *we* interpret, doesn't belong there. What we don't see, or understand, becomes extraneous and affects our way of thinking. We become troubled, displaced, unsettled in our daily living. Some turn to drink," he says as he turned and looked straight into Scott's eyes. "I think you're interpreting these dreams as demonic and try to justify them by telling yourself, for example, you're over worked." This time he was looking directly at Chris. "You want to distance yourself from them and even wish they belonged to someone else," he says as he faced Lou. "Well gentlemen, they won't go away. Stop resisting and let them flow to see where it takes you. You will see your own future. So, let us wait and see what lies before you."

Three Dreams

"Brilliant minds, representing a variety of approaches, are taking part in this project. They're the best science has to offer, and will be with you, as I will, every step of the way. According to our data you have given positive indication of integrative experiences in these 'visions'...and that's what they are, put simply, visions. Our results indicate this event may, very soon, come to pass. Where? How? When or even why remains a mystery. We think, very soon. You are predicting the future gentlemen."

Dr Ito was so emphatic that he gave the impression that he knew something they didn't...that he had some project already shaped in his mind. Lou and Chris were unsure if they should be grateful or resistant to what they were about to encounter.

To Scott, his words brought the image of a gypsy, reading a crystal ball in a sideshow, and 'predicting the future' for quarters.

"Like a dang fortune teller," he burst out, leaping from his chair, his Adams apple bobbing in his throat. "I want to know the truth."

Chris pulled him back into his seat and "Whispered, "Let him finish. Did you really expect these people to have instant answers?"

"No, not exactly," added the other man who had been silently listening, while nodding his head in affirmation throughout. "I'm Doctor Stone, a colleague of Dr Isu and Dr Malik." His hand moved automatically to the small of his back where he pressed the spine into submission to keep him erect.

"My theory—and it is a theory, but strongly supported by scientific research, is that this is certainly a phenomenon...a once-in-a-life-time occurrence. None of you have shown any indication of having had ESP previously, except for Scott, and it is unlikely you will in the future. You, unlike fortunetellers, are not charlatans! You are actually perceiving something, we believe, that will indeed, come to pass."

"Oliver Docks once said, *'the truth is sort of a mystery and sometimes has nothing to do with fact.'* He spoke as though the phrase had special meaning for him. "We shall soon know the truth."

His hand moved quickly from his back and jutted up to scratch his ear, circling his finger within.

As he returned to his seat, he hesitated, as if he had forgotten something. He stood for a moments, then added, "These dreams or precognition usually arrive near to the event. I'd say it could happen within a very few days…yes, yes…a very few days. Actually, it could be tonight." Looking pleased, he then eased himself into the chair.

Dr Ito formed his fingers into a steeple. He glared at Dr Stone in silence, obviously disturbed by the interruption.

Dr Stone remained mute, apparently remembering Dr Ito's temperament.

"It can't happen soon enough to suit me." Scott murmured under his breath.

Chris marshaled his thoughts.

"May I ask how you came to that conclusion, doctor," he asked, groping for threads of hope.

"We have a great deal of experience in being able to determine which ESP experiences *are* precognition and, which are merely *thought* to be precognition," Ito continued, glancing at Stone, as if awaiting his commentary on this intelligence.

"The chronology of events, test results, and data corroborate our belief in these events. Other unknown events will occur in a matter of days. Each has something that connects you to it and each other…that will move this toward its ultimate end. You were *selected.* This did not happen randomly. A tiger can kill an elephant if it bites him once a day."

Before they could respond, the team was gone.

"The hell with it…let's get drunk," Scott said melodiously, in an attempt to lighten their dismal mood. "Moping ain't getting us anywhere."

Lapsing into silence, they headed for Leo's place.

11: 20 a.m. June 5

During the fifteen-minute drive, each wove himself an ingenious web of probabilities, the surest shield a man can place between himself and the probable truth. Each was lost in his own imagination. They built a scenario of how the disaster might occur, each turning over the possibilities in his mind. How? When? Where? Questions with no answers galloped through their psyche…the mystery mixed with reality, of what was forthcoming.

Chris imagined the disaster would occur during a storm.

Lou visualized two ships colliding in a fog.

Scott thought about an explosion from within the cargo hold. Maybe some chemicals or something.

Pulling up to the bar, Chris knew Cuppy and Sky were already inside. His Land Rover and her Jeep were parked at the curb in front. He pulled in behind them.

Entering, Scott recognized two buddies he knew near the pool table. With a yell and a wave, he moved in their direction.

Lazy grayish-blue smoke hung low in the airless room. Lou's fellow shipmates were sitting at the same table, drinking beer, where Chris first met them. When they spotted them entering, they waved them over.

Chris's stomach felt like two squirrels on an exercise wheel, and he really wasn't in the mood for company. He asked Lou to thank them, but declined. As he walked to the bar he could hear them launching questions at Lou, one after another.

While Sky waited for him she played with the olive in-between sips of her now dwindling martini. When he approached, she smiled and patted the stool next to her.

He slumped into the stool, then propped his knee against the bar. "I need a drink."

Sky, recognizing the basement gloom in the set of his shoulders, waved to Leo. Catching his eye, she motioned to him to bring Chris a drink.

"We didn't accomplish a thing…not a thing," he volunteered. "Doctor Isu and his colleagues think this…this thing, hasn't happened yet, but will…soon. They're convinced it's a prediction or something. I'm not sure it is."

Sky was his best friend, his lover, and his advisor. These past years she had provided, at appropriate times, encouragement, criticism (sometimes ruthlessly), advice and praise. He wondered why he didn't turn to her now. Perhaps because there are some things she just couldn't fix. Sometimes some things were out of both of their control. Pent in his memory was a reminder not to discuss the matter with her since she was, to say the least, skeptical and gave no credence to 'the dream thing.'

"Dr. Isu?"

"Yes. Apparently he's the top dog in this research. Quite brilliant, from what I gather."

"Is that all they told you? What about the tests? Didn't they find anything?"

"In essence that's all there is. The tests only confirmed that we're sharing the exact same dreams and that they're predictions, which they feel, will come true. When? Where? How? No one knows. It's getting to me. Before they were just nightmares. Now the nightmares are turning into some strange future event, or so they say." There was no belief in his voice, only confusion.

"Well darling, could that be so bad? She tried to make her questions as nonthreatening as possible.

Silence. He felt like a rubber band someone had stretched too far. Right now, he wanted to push time, make it march to a quicker drum.

"Did they say how you three are involved? I mean…there must be a connection, or else why would the three of you be experiencing the same thing?"

The shrug she came to know lately returned. Staring at the mirror, but seeing nothing, he sat in silence. He held his drink firmly between his two hands as if it were going to jump up and run away from him.

"So, what do we do now," she asked with false calm. Her voice sounded tired, as though she felt the strain more than he did.

His hand shot up and waved her questions aside. He thought there were some things he wanted to keep private.

Sky found her cheeks burning with color and thought about leaving, but didn't. She gave him a glance that would have withered him on the spot, had he seen it. She tucked her hair behind her ears, smiled with an effort of will, and then reached out to touch his arm.

He started to withdraw, but when he caught a glimpse of himself in the mirror, he stopped. Her face registered something he couldn't identify: it wasn't good. He was ashamed with the way he treated her. She didn't deserve it. "I shouldn't have done that. I guess I'm not in the mood for conversation, right now," he apologized without retreating an inch, although his eyes were completely guarded. "Just give me a little time, will ya?"

Her body stiffened. Her face fell immediately. She opened her mouth, but no words came out. Her thoughts, stillborn. Chris, who had seemed so near to her only a short time before, was distant and cold now. She felt separated from him. She wanted to crawl inside of him and curl around his heart, to protect him, but he was having none of it. He had changed over these past months and she was afraid she was losing him. The thought made her ache. *It's all because of those damn dreams,* she thought. *We were fine until they started. What's happening to us?*

She saw him watching her through the mirror and tried to smile through lips that trembled. Choosing her words as carefully as a diplomat visiting a foreign country, as asked, "Where do we go from here Chris?"

Surprised, he turned to look in her eyes. Leo calling his name broke the cavernous, thunderous silence that followed.

"Chris...Chris. Telephone," he says, holding up the receiver.

Reluctantly Chris unfolded himself from the stool and ambled down the bar, pausing only, to say a word or two to a burly man at the bar.

"Hello?"

Pause.

"How did it get out? Who?"

"What? What," he asked angrily.

Concerned, Sky glanced down the bar at him.

Silence fell over the room. The jukebox, as if on cue, ceased playing. The only sounds in the room came from the humming of the overhead fans.

"Jesus Christ! Thanks! Thanks a lot Steve." With that he slammed down the telephone. What he heard hit him like a rock in the chest. He paced nervously back and forth for a few moments, then leaned his head against the wall, clenched his eyes shut, and tried to calm himself down.

Unable to contain his rage, he put his fist through the wall and was momentarily surprised by the heat of his anger.

Sky jumped off her stool and sped to his side.

"What is it? Tell me...what is it Chris? What's the matter? I've never seen you this way. You're scaring me. What is it," she pleaded, with far less fear than she felt inside. Her unblinking eyes were at first, glued on the hole in the wall, then onto his eyes. She had never seen Chris this angry. He was not a violent man. She kept her voice calm, her eyes burning into his.

Ignoring her, he scanned the room, searching for Lou, Cuppy and Scott. It was then that he noticed Cuppy in deep conversation with Lou. They were engrossed over papers that were sprawled across the table, and seemed oblivious of his outbreak.

"Lou...Cup," he called. When they looked up, he motioned them over.

Scott was staring at him from across the room and was already moving in his direction. Chris waved him over too.

As they approached, he turned and walked outside. Sky was right on Lou's heels.

It took a few moments for their eyes to become adjusted to the bright sunlight.

"What's up," Cup says, shading his hand above his eyes.

"Musta been something real bad. I never seen him so mad," said Scott as he scurried out the door. Sky followed in hot pursuit.

Chris stood with his hands on his hips and looked at each of them.

"We've got trouble. The media has gotten hold of this," he says, in outraged anger.

Sky's eyes widened in astonishment. "You mean there's a leak...that someone told the media?" She shook her head in disbelief.

"Well who the hell told them," Scott screamed. **"Shit...shit!"**

"I don't know. I just got a call from Steve. He denied being the source of the leak. Said our files were missing and that he had a suspect or two, but couldn't prove which one of them absconded with them. He said the media came to his office looking for us but he didn't tell them anything."

"Then how did they find out," Scott repeated, in a voice that could be heard a block away.

"Cripes...they'll have a frenzy. Now what," Lou muttered.

"One thing's for sure, they'll bend this story to suit themselves. God knows *what* they'll make us out to be," Chris says.

"So what'll we do now," says Lou quietly, shoving his hands in his pockets.

Sky finally recovered from the news, and suggested they go over to Chris's place, and work out what they were going to do next.

1:10 p.m. June 5

Everyone piled into their cars. Lou and Sky rode with Chris.

As they turned the corner of Chris's street, they saw TV vans parked all along his street. Half way down the block, they spotted a bank of reporters milling around outside his house. Cameras were already situated on tripods, sound men had microphones, and reporters had their tape recorders ready, awaiting their arrival. When they spotted their car coming, they broke into frenzy and began rushing toward them.

"Mr. Healy, Mr. Healy...."

"Quick, down the alley," says Sky. "When we get to the back door, make a run for it."

Chris jerked the wheel to the right, sending all the occupants to the opposite corner. The tires crunched noisily on the gravel as they spun into the alley with Cuppy only inches behind him. The car stopped abruptly at his back door. He put it in park and killed the motor. They leapt from their cars, lifted their knees in swift leaps, and dove for the door. Chris could smell the salty dampness in the air as his hand tightened on the doorknob.

Everyone quickly piled inside, escaping the cameras of the paparazzi.

"Now I know how Diana felt with those paparazzi chasing her down for a photo," says Lou.

Chris flipped on the TV as soon as they entered while Sky headed for the kitchen to make sandwiches and coffee.

"Let's see if we've made the latest news," he said sarcastically, and then lowered him into the recliner across from the screen. It was not his nature to be sarcastic. He had reason to be sarcastic now.

Cuppy and Scott lowered themselves onto the couch while Lou leaned up against the wall. Sky pulled up another chair and sat down.

"**...We here at KKYC wish him well. Now ladies and gentlemen, here's a human interest story.**"

Susan Blake, a reporter for the KKYC, was reporting from outside the National Oceanic and Atmospheric Administration building. She was holding a dildo shaped microphone that was covered with some sort of fuzzy material. Cuppy thought it looked like a penis that was stolen off of an old camel.

"...Radio and TV stations have been inundated with phone calls asking for more information about the three men who allegedly have a premonition of the sinking of a cruise ship, where, *they say*, among the wreckage, will be a lone survivor—-an infant. Sources say, Doctors Chris Healy and Scott Spencer, who work here at the National Oceanic and Atmospheric Administration, in Honolulu, are predicting some rather strange, yet bizarre events. Our source tells us they *dreamed* that an ocean liner would go down, or has already sunk, and there would be a lone survivor...a small child." The reporter smirked. "The Coast Guard informs us that all ships are presently accounted for. We could not get any comment from the from Dr Healy and Dr Spencer, but their Public Relations Officer tells us that it is very unlikely that these prominent doctors would make such damaging statements. If true, perhaps Drs Healey and Spencer could tell us where to locate this mythical ship. Back to you Tom."

Like a Cobra getting ready to strike, Scott rose from his chair and stared at the reporter condescendingly. "That bitch. That no good son of a bitch. Where does she get off...? Now everyone's gonna think we're nuts...three loony tunes. People are gonna be asking us to find their lost dogs, or the like. I'd like to kill someone. Shit, shit." He gave her the middle finger of his right hand. "Here, sit on this baby. She's going to milk this for everything it's worth. Our reputations have just gone out the window...and it's all because of you, you bitch." Suddenly he was startled, and embarrassed at his outburst, though the newscaster couldn't possibly have heard him.

His bluntness was enough to unsettle Sky. "I don't want to hear any more. This is turning into a circus," said Sky as she turns off the set.

"Cripes, where do think they got their info? I've heard of gossip traveling fast, but this fast," breathed Cuppy.

Everyone was quiet. From the front of the house came sounds of car doors slamming and unintelligible voices, all chattering at once.

Scott," Cuppy says.

"What?"

"Your mouth...you're catching flies."

Scott slammed his mouth shut and smiled self-consciously.

"We can't blame her. Some asshole gave her the information and probably made a bundle doing it. You don't suppose that asshole is Steve, do you," says Cuppy.

"No, not hardly.

"Well, we've had it. At least they didn't mention *your* name," Chris said sullenly, looking over at Lou.

"It's only a matter of time. They've got their teeth into this thing and aren't going to let go. Chances are they already know who I am. Right now, I'm not as important as two doctors are. Just wait and see. Soon I'll be hanging from the yard arm right along side of ya."

He held in his hand a notebook scrawled with notes and figures, which he continued to write in. Cuppy pointed to something within while he whispered close to Lou's ear. The rest of them wondered what they were up to.

"Did you ever see the likes of this," Sky said, still staring at the black screen. She shot a bewildered glance around the room as panic whelmed up inside. 'What if it doesn't happen? What if it does? Poor Chris. What is he going to do now?'

"Anyone got any suggestions," Chris asks sullenly.

"Well ole buddy, I wouldn't show my face outside for a while," Cuppy says, with a quick smile.

Suddenly there was a knock on the door.

"Don't answer that," says Sky, "it's probably those reporters."

"Look out to see who it is," says Chris.

Cuppy peeked through the drape. A lone man stood on the stoop, smoking a cigarette. He waved back at him with one hand, and reached to the back pocket of his trousers with the other and withdrew a leather wallet. He held up an ID card that Cuppy couldn't read in the dim light.

"Some man. Can't tell who it is, but he's alone." Glancing over to the reporters, he noted they were standing there quietly, watching the visitor at the door. He thought that peculiar. "What do you want me to do? Let him in?"

"Not till I know who it is, and what he wants," Chris said, moving toward the door. He opened it a crack. "If you're a reporter, forget it. There's no story here."

A hand with blunt fingers shot in the door holding an open wallet, exposing a PRESS PASS identification card, behind a tattered plastic pocket. "Please give me a minute...just one minute. If you do I'll get rid of them out there," said the muffled voice.

Everyone stood up and hesitantly moved closer to the door, to see whom the stranger was.

Chris nodded an okay and Cuppy stepped back from the door so that he could enter.

The man in the doorway wore a suit that appeared to be clean, but looked like it had been hand washed. It was wrinkled and hung on him like a suit that was a size too large. The white shirt underneath was unbuttoned at the neck and appeared more wrinkled than the suit. The faded tie that was draped around his neck hung limply above his seasoned belt. Self-consciously, he reached back and stuffed his shirt into his pants.

There were small traces of fatigue around his reddened eye sockets. He looked tired. Not physically tired, but deflated tired. Chris saw the pain behind them and suspected it had been there for many years. His 5'8" bulky frame gave a hint that he was, at one time, athletic. His graying hair was neatly combed and appeared to have been recently cut.

Phil McDowell was formerly a journalist of great intellectual depth. His critically acclaimed articles, exposing the truth about veterans returning from battle, earned him a nomination for the Pulitzer Prize. His career reflected his tenacity for knocking down a story and his desire to expose improprieties, to make them right. His exceptional talent and journalistic ethics had earned him the respect from noted journalists on five continents, many of with whom he had collaborated.

Three years ago his columns began, slowly at first, to be riddled with inaccuracies, half-truths, flaws, and contradictions. If he didn't get *this* story, his career was over. His editor was on the verge of firing him.

After marrying his childhood sweetheart in Texas, they moved to Hawaii where he took a position with the *Honolulu Gazette*. They tried to become pregnant for four years but began to think it hopeless. On their fifth wedding anniversary they learned they were going to have a child. Both were thrilled beyond words.

Unexpectedly Scott received a vision about this man standing before him. It initially focused on Phil working on a piece for his editor and time was running out. Phil stretched, looked at his watch, and then moved toward the nursery.

A little girl, five pounds, seven ounces, was born on an early August morning. She was named after his wife's favorite flower, Rose. Phil loved her so much that he'd call home several times a day to check on her progress. He was more than willing to baby-sit, bathe her; change diapers, and bored everybody to death with endless snapshots of his 'little angel.' It was while he was home alone with Rose that disaster struck. It was to change the trajectory of his life.

Scott saw him going into to Rose's room to check on her after putting together, and before calling in, an article for the morning edition. He cringed when he saw him pick up the infant. When his wife came home from visiting her parents, she peeked into the baby's room, where she knew she would find him. There he was, singing a lullaby, while rocking their daughter in an old oak rocking chair. Immediately the hair stood up on the back of her neck, although she really didn't understand why, she knew something was definitely wrong.

She smiled as she stepped into the room, where she found him singing softly against their baby's tiny shell-like ear.

"Hi honey. Hi baby girl." He could hear the affection in her voice.

Then the smile disappeared and was replaced with alarm when she saw tears streaming down his cheeks. She had never seen him cry before. Her heart began to race. She moved closer.

Scott watched in despair.

"Phil…what's wrong?" Fear crept into her voice like secretive thieves in the night.

He continued singing between sobs.

"Phil…tell me, what's wrong?"

Again, he ignored her.

She was trembling as she moved closer to pull the pink blanket aside. Phil sharply grabbed her wrist and pushed her away with such force, that she fell to the floor. Fear raced through her mind. Her eyes darted from the baby to Phil, to the baby again. The infant wasn't moving. His singing took on a mournful sound. On her knees beside him, she softly pleaded with him to give her the baby. After what seemed like eons, but in reality were only a few minutes, he finally allowed her to take the still child.

He began to scream, "**No, no, nooo!**"

Three Dreams

To her horror, their child was dead.

Shocked, Scott sucked in his breath and was jolted back to reality. '*My God, the poor man. What a burden to carry,*' he thought. He wanted to give Phil his sympathies, but decided against it when he saw the heavy sorrow standing in his eyes. He jammed his hands into his pocket to hide his own trembling. He was breathing as if he'd been running.

Although little was known about it at the time, Doctors determined it was a crib death. Phil blamed himself for not looking in on her sooner and more often. Assurance by Doctors that these deaths were unexplainable, he blamed himself and stayed in seclusion for several months. Her death seemed to weigh on him as much as the collected sins of the world. His wife thought a burden shared is a burden divided in half, and tried to cling to him in their grief. To no avail. His pain only found solace in drink.

Without warning Scott was jolted forward in time, to the day of the funeral. He saw Phil remove a rose from the spray of flowers on the tiny white casket, and then drop it in a small transparent sleeve. He placed it in his wallet, and then dropped it into his suit pocket next to his heart. It would be a reminder of his lost angel. The vision faded.

He glanced over in time to see the withered rose contained within the yellowed cellophane that had been carefully placed in his worn wallet. He knew Phil still hadn't banished his pain and sadness. He could only contain it. It was straight up noticeable how quickly grief dulled his looks, as rapidly as any illness.

Suddenly he was brought back to the present, visibly shaken.

As the intruder, hungry for a story, cleared his throat, he closed his wallet and dropped it in the inside pocket of his jacket. His blue eyes skipped around the room. "My name is Phil McDowell. I'm a reporter with the *Honolulu Gazette*. Those are my friends out there," he says, as he punched a thumb over his shoulder. "They elected me to come in here and get *your* side of the story. We want, very much, to set the record straight."

"We have no story," spat Sky. "Why don't you get out," she said as she moved toward the door.

"Everyone has a story. Yours is already out. Everyone loves a mystery. Me? I hate any attempt to mystify. The public is captivated by stories that reveal cowardice or heroism. They're drawn to the human drama of the story itself. Some will be drawn to this so-called rescue of innocence...remember baby Jessica in Texas several years ago? Think people didn't care? Think again. If you lay everything on the line with me, then I'll piecemeal it out to the media. They don't have to know *everything*...besides, they'll have a field day if you don't give them some answers," he says matter-of-factly. "They'll print *anything* that'll sell papers, even if they do embellish a little. They may depict you unfairly or even inaccurately...for color, you might say. Which would you rather have," he says as he glances around the room, "all of them or one of me? There's a seedbed of imaginations germinating out there. Think what they could do. I'm here to get the truth. If there's nothing to it, okay. We'll all go away. But if there is, people have the right to know."

Lou, who had been leaning against the wall, fixed his eyes on him with the kind of look one would reserve for a child molester.

"You made a mistake," he snapped. "Two, in fact. First, there is no story. Second, we'll deny everything, no matter what you print...and then we'll sue you."

"Of course, you could do that. What then? What do you think they'll do? Stop and just go away because you denied it? I'm afraid not. The scandalmongers already have you typecast. They'll haunt you to your grave. The press is like a dog with a bone and they won't let go until they know everything you know."

He reached into his inside pocket and pulled out a stack of Xeroxed papers.

"Before you think about suing, I think you should see these." He handed Chris the papers, then calmly walked over to the nearest chair and slumped into it.

Hesitantly, Chris took the papers. Everyone but Lou gathered around to see what it was. Copies. Copies of their confidential medical records' straight from Steve's office!

"Where the hell did you get these," Chris asks angrily.

Lou shot across the room and grabbed them out of his hand. His curious eyes examined several copies.

Scott pulled out a few pages, while Cuppy and Sky looked over their shoulders.

"Jesus, Mary and Joseph, we're screwed," says Lou, eyes flashing with anger. Fuming, he tore the sheets to shreds, and threw them at Phil.

"Prove it," he spat.

Three Dreams

Phil watched them with the dutiful attention of a bored but courteous observer. A smirk passed over his lips. *These guys are phony,* he thought. *They're playing their parts well; I'll have to give them that. Well, if they're unscrupulous con artists, I'll find out, and quick.* He sat forward, fascinated by their 'shock.' He thought they played their roles well.

Scott threw his papers to the floor, looking like he'd received a body blow.

"We've had it, no matter where he got 'em." He collapsed into the armchair, shaking his back and forth in disbelief. His arms and legs hung like a discarded puppet, still grasping one of the pages. "Shit. What are we gonna do now," he said, shaking the crumbled page in the air.

"Why don't you go paper your living room with them, if you love them so much," Sky asks, glaring at him. Her head bobbed up and down emphatically. Her earrings followed in agreement.

"How many people have copies," Chris asks, looking concerned as he continued reading.

"May as well tell ya. You're gonna find out eventually. The prominent doctor has, or rather, had a secretary who loves money. As far as I know, the only other set is in my safe. Unfortunately, prying eyes opened it, minutes before I got there. I think I got them all, but who knows how many copies are floating around that I don't know about? Through various sources this story, with all its details, and other picturesque additions, will come pouring out. They think it's good stuff, a variable scoop, and they're going to run with it. I'm interested in getting your side of it. Can we talk about it?" Pause. "I won't print a word if you don't want me to...I swear." Smiling, he reached into his left pocket and pulled out a small writing tablet, then reached into the right one and retrieved a pen. Sitting back he crossed his legs, then waited.

"You mean it was," says Cuppy menacing. His face was beet red. His hands were clenched, ready to hit someone or something.

"His secretary," Lou interrupted.

Chris's hand flew to his forehead. He stared into nothingness, shaking his head back and forth.

Scott paced back and forth. "I knew I didn't trust that bitch. We'll sue. We'll sue the whole damn bunch of them. That's confidential information…between doctor and patient. We'll sue for everything they're worth."

Sky knew Phil's casualness irritated everyone in the room. She read the mocking challenge behind his smile. It was as if he didn't believe a word of it and already knew they couldn't do anything, but cooperate. She wondered why she was so protective when she thought it was a Red Herring as well.

With everyone having copies of their records, she knew they couldn't much deny what they had experienced. The question was, how *much* should they reveal? How much would pacify the public? Many will think they're crazy, hallucinating, or God knows what else. This had to be handled with utmost delicacy, by everyone. Religious nuts were probably already erecting shrines to them, coworkers would be scoffing at them, and jokes would be passed around bars across the country, if not, around the world. *Did ya hear the one about…?* She shuddered with the thought of what might come.

"Ya, I bet. You want to sell papers like those people out there. You'll turn this into a circus," says Sky, folding her arms across her chest.

Everyone was too shocked to speak.

"Well, I don't see that we have any choice. How can we be assured that you're not going to run with this…blow it out of proportion? What assurance do we have that it's not going to be all over the papers tomorrow…disjointed and out of context? How can we be sure we can trust you," Chris says leaning into Phil's face.

"Now come on," says Cuppy cynically, "no reporter can be trusted, especially with the truth."

Standing, Phil gave a disproving cluck and waved his finger at him. "You don't know, but I'm a man of my word. Most certainly it will be in this evening's edition and you know they're already on TV, but I'll be up front with you Mr. Healy," he says turning to Chris. "I don't believe a word of it! I want to put this story down. I think there's a hidden agenda behind all this and I'm going to get to the bottom of it, or die trying. So, if you want all this hoopla to go away, then you'll tell me about those records." He slid back into a chair, and then jotted something in his notebook. He had every intention of keeping a detailed record of everything that was said by these people. There was no doubt his editor was going to have a myriad of questions later and he wanted to be ready.

Three Dreams

Still heated, Lou didn't want any part of this flippant newspaperman. He'd rather be tinkering in his shop. "I'm getting out of here. You tell him what you want. I'm behind you," says Lou. "Can I catch a ride from you Cuppy?"

"Yeah, sure." Cuppy reached over and removed a sandwich from the tray, took a bite, and strode toward the back door while glaring at the unwelcome guest.

"See ya later," says Scott.

"Ya buddy, see ya," says Cuppy, not taking his eyes off of Phil. He then turned and left.

"Well, I'd...I'd best get goin' too," says Scott, looking uncomfortable. "Marlene will be worried. Call me." He paused, as if he had something more to say, but thinking twice, decided against it. After taking a sandwich for himself, he left.

Everyone else sat quietly.

The pager on Chris's belt began pulsating. The number indicated it was Paul Brown, his boss. He picked up the receiver.

It was no surprise to him when the first words out of his mouth were, "what the hell is going on?" His voice was at a pitch that rivaled a bomb exploding next to his ear.

"The goddamn media is camped on our doorstep. They're trying to beat down the doors. They think you're the ones who are behind all of this shit. After all," he said sarcastically, "two of my best men are causing all the brouhaha. So what is it? Looking for publicity? More money? What? Worried about fame or infamy? The media is going to trying to chew you up and have your carcasses for lunch. So what, what is it? What the hell is going on Chris? This is not like you. If there's any iota of truth here the media might even outdo themselves from the Simpson case." You ought to see it out here. It's a regular circus. I had to call the cops for mob control...there's lookey-loos everywhere. It's that bad." There was such a long pause that followed, that Chris thought the conversation was over and started to hang up.

"Look Chris," he said softly. "I know you...and I know 'the genius.' I know you two didn't have anything to do with this...it's not like you...either of you. Dreams...a baby alive in a shipwreck. Boy, where do they get them," he chuckled.

"It's preposterous but I have to give them credit for their imaginative imaginations. I wonder where they dug that one up though. Meanwhile these fools are camped outside and ain't leavin' till we offer a press release."

Chris wanted to say something, but the words wouldn't come. He thought it better if he had a one-on-one with Paul. He was a decent man. Perhaps he'd understand. He hoped he would.

"I'll be there within the hour Paul. I'll tell you everything then. Can't do it over the phone."

"See me the minute you get here," he insisted. "However, you may be receiving a call from me sooner than that. We're getting a lot of activity, about 110 miles off of the Kiwi Channel. Looks like a new fault might be opening up. And we're also seeing some activity 80 miles further southwest from there. Nothing to worry about right now…just some rumbling. I've got to go. Talk to you later."

"Yes sir," says Chris, cradling the phone.

"Your boss," Phil asks.

"Yes."

"Mad eh?"

"To say the least." He stuck his thumbs in his belt, and began to formulate what he was going to tell Paul, without him throwing him out of his office, or rushing him off to a psychiatrist.

Sky, now draped over the chair, was silently watching. She thought it best not to say anything and let Chris decide what he wanted to do, alone.

Chris eased himself onto the couch and put his feet up on the coffee table. He folded his hands behind his head and stared up at watermark on the ceiling. *'I don't even know where to start,'* he thought. *Guess what, boss, Scott and I had a dream, and, oh yeah, so did another guy. Yes Paul, it's all true…maybe! The three of us had congruent dreams, 'and yes, there is a child alive below…maybe. Yeah, right! I'll be looking for a new job tomorrow. Oh brother.* His eyes narrowed and his stomach flipped when he thought of standing in the unemployment office…right next to Scott. *Could all this be a conspiracy*, he wondered.

Noting the silence, he glanced over at Sky, as if to make sure she was still there, then over to Phil who was writing furiously in his tablet.

She learned early in their relationship that the rational level of her mind wasn't always on the most useful level when he was in this mood. She still wasn't convinced about the dreams, the child, Lou, and all the rest. She thought it would play itself out one way or another, eventually.

Abruptly the vision of the woman flashed before him again. For some reason this time he was transfixed by the image.

"Come now. Time is running out. Save her." He had never given any thought to the sex of the child before, but was mildly pleased it was a girl. The mother's hair was wetter and now matted to her face. He could see her clothes saturated and stuck to her body. She beckoned for him to come. He shut his eyes tightly and shook his head, in an attempt to shake off the image. When he opened them again she was still there. He knew that face...but from where? Something about her teased his recollection. He wracked his brain to remember.

Seeing the look on his face, Phil leaned toward Chris. His eyes narrowed. It was obvious that something was going on. Chris tilted his head as if he were straining to hear something or someone, in the distance. He was intensely absorbed by the vision.

"What is it Chris," he asked, as if he were afraid to hear the answer. His eyes darted around the room, the back to Chris.

The vision evaporated. Shaken, Chris rose and went to the refrigerator. He pulled out a beer, snapped the top off with his thumb, and gulped half the bottle down before his stomach drowned the butterflies. Strolling back into the living room, he half whispered, not understanding it himself, "It's her again."

"Who," says Phil, throwing a wondering glance at Sky.

"The woman in my visions. "I don't know who she is," he insisted, "but I do know I've seen her before. Just where or when has eluded me." He felt a tug at his memory, a strain. There was something familiar about her. His brain raced over the places he'd been the people he'd met in the past, but came up with nothing.

"What woman? What visions," says Sky, surprised. "Chris, you're beginning to scare me." She jutted forward, awaiting an answer.

"I've been having these...these visions...twice before...and she's appeared in the dreams. She has long red hair and always looks like she just crawled out of the ocean. I think it's the mother and she's trying to tell me something. I can't make out what it is. She vanishes before I can find out. Don't ask me any more about her. I just don't know anything else. I didn't tell you before because no one else had seen her and I didn't want you to think she was a fantasy or a wish-fulfillment."

"Would you mind telling me what you're talking about," says Phil.

Chris thought for a few minutes. He didn't want to sound like he was hallucinating or that he was a pathological liar scratching for attention. He contemplated telling Phil the whole story. He knew he had to tell him something…only what…how much. He decided to tell him all and only hoped he would do what was right with the information. Careers could be ruined.

"Okay, I'm going to have to trust you."

Phil sat back in his seat. *Ah, here it comes. Blarney. Come on; give it to me buddy. I'm ready. He must think 'm some sort of sucker. Okay, shoot.*

He told him the story from beginning to end. Phil sat there stunned. It was too implausible, too unbelievable. He fought within himself to reject what he just heard, but a part of him wanted to believe, because of the infant. His mind flashed back to when he couldn't save his own child. If true, perhaps he can help save this one. He thought he'd try one more stratagem to see if Chris was on the level.

"So, when does the ship go down," Phil asked almost inaudibly.

Neither could make out what he said. "What," asked Chris.

"When does the God damn ship sink?" Phil was testing them. He waited for an answer.

Surprised and startled by the direct question, Chris leapt to his feet and leaned over the reporter. Shoving his thumb toward the door, he spat, "Why the hell don't you get out of here? What are you anyway, a ghoul? Can't wait for a tragedy for a scoop? Do you realize how many people might die? We don't know where or when, or even what ship…just that we think there may be one survivor…maybe," he shouted.

The two men glared at each other for several moments.

Phil then dropped his gaze and extended his hand. "Thanks son, that's all I needed to know," he said softly. *I wasn't sure if you guys were weirdoes or what, but I can now see you really do believe in this stuff. It all sounded wishy-washy to me but I'm totally convinced you're telling the truth, as you know it. There are lots of B.S. artists out there. I had to know. You understand that, don't you?'

Three Dreams

"I've had some experience in this area and I've found that paranormal abilities are not the creation of con men and hucksters but are real events that happen to real people. The paranormal can't be believed or disbelieved. Sure, earlier in this century, believing in dreams smacked vaguely of mental or emotional disorders. Now? Now people are more educated in these things. Perhaps that's why everyone wants to know if this is for real. If it is, it would be a miracle and the world could use a miracle or two right now."

"You boys gotta see this thing through, if for no other reason than to see where it leads. You were given the dreams for a reason. Let's face it they can't be coincidences. If they're exactly alike, doesn't it make you wonder? Why it's you guys is anybody's guess. I feel strongly that it's you Chris who has to be there when…if…there's a recovery. I don't know why I know, but you do. I should have my head examined…getting involved in something like this. Who'd ever believe a story like this?" He stood and headed for the bathroom. He stopped, put his hand on the back of his head, turned and said, "I would!"

Chris wondered how Phil could do an about face so fast. He sat down and placed his elbows on his knees and held his head between his hands. He wished he could believe as much as Phil did, but he didn't. *Maybe it's a fluke*, he thought. *This thing is getting out of hand.* He wanted to brain that secretary.

"So what about this woman. I didn't hear anyone else mention her."

"He told you that no one else has seen see her."

"Do you know her? Who is she? Why does she appear only to you?"

"That face, I know that face." He conjured her up in his mind's eye, trying to remember. His brain raced through the places he'd been, and the people he'd met again.

"Where…." Chris sprang to his feet. His eyes lit up. Snapping his fingers he says jubilantly, "I've got it!" The look on his face was like that of a child who had cooked breakfast for his parents for the first time.

"What is it Chris," Sky asked excitedly. "What do you remember?" She clapped her hands in glee.

"Wait," he said with a smile and rushed to the bedroom. They could hear drawers opening and closing. Finally he emerged from the room holding up a medallion that was dangling from a chain.

"Do you remember this?"

Looking up, Sky frowned.

Phil moved closer to the edge of his seat.

"Remember? Japan? The dancer? The red headed dancer?" he emphasized. I told you about it. Remember? I think it's a medal for mariners, or sailors, or something to do with the sea. Saint...saint...saint...."

Leaping up, "Elmo," says Phil, caught up in the excitement.

"I told you about it...how I got it."

"No, actually you didn't. You passed it off, at the time. Said you'd tell me later. You were in a hurry. Remember?"

"Oh? I thought I had. I'd forgotten all about it...all this time."

They all stared at the medal as if it were about to speak.

"So tell us, how did you get it," asked Phil, almost bursting with curiosity.

Chris thought for a minute. "I was on my way to a speaking engagement at a conference in Japan. On the way there a parade blocked the cab's route, so I decided to walk the rest of the way. The colors...the people, thousands of them. When I stopped to watch the parade, a dancer appeared before me. She smiled, then took my hand, and pressed the medal into my palm. I thought that it was a token...what all the dancers gave the onlookers along the sidelines, so I slipped it into my pocket. I didn't think anything about it until it fell out when you were packing my jacket...remember?"

"It was her...the mother. Her red hair was showing under the headdress. I remember that clearly." He paused for a few moments, trying to remember more. "She said...she said as she closed my fingers around it, 'Come to the twelve moon seas,' or something like that. Maybe she said, 'I'm June and I'll see you in the sea.' No, that's not it. Christ, I can't remember...all that noise...it was hard to hear. I really didn't pay that much attention, or not enough to believe it meant anything." Pausing again, he added, "Come to think of it, I don't remember seeing anyone else around me getting one. Anyway, she melted into the crowd and I never saw her again"

"What's a Christian medal doing at a Japanese festival," Phil asked, turning away. He tapped his pen against his forehead, and then blew out a breath. "Curious."

"Don't you think you should call someone…the doctor, Steve…someone," says Sky.

"Later."

Turning back, Phil raised his pen toward them, as if he was going to say something.

"You never said if she was oriental."

"No. No, she wasn't."

"Had you seen her before that day?"

"No, not that I can remember…but then again, that red hair…. I can remember seeing that red-gold hair against the sun. It was as if she knew me. She looked right into my eyes, as if she hadn't seen me for a long time, but I don't remember ever meeting her before." His eyes narrowed as he tried to recall. "Something about that hair keeps tugging at the back of my mind. When I got back, I stuck the medal in the drawer and never gave it another thought…until today."

Sky took the medallion from Chris and brought it to the light for a better look.

"Maybe the mother gave birth to the child on the cruise…before she went down…maybe she's still trying to save it. Apparitions have appeared to people before. Maybe this is one of them. She's asking you specifically to save her child and is pleading for you to come," says Phil, digging deeply for answers.

"Come to where for Christ sake. Where?"

Roberta M. Alleman

3:30 p.m. June 5

When the phone rang, it startled them two inches off the floor. It rang only once. Then stopped. "That's Scott's signal." He turned and picked up the phone, touching the #3 speed-dial button.

Chris picked up the phone on the first ring.

"I saw it. Tidal waves," Scott screamed in his ear. "Two giant tidal waves, like you ain't ever seen before." I saw them...I saw them. It's happened...the ship going down...seawater ripping through the gaping holes...bulkheads snapping like twigs...emergency sirens blaring...people screaming...of God Chris, it's happening. It's happening right now...this very minute. My God, those poor people. They had nowhere to hide...they were at the mercy of...." He was sobbing loudly. He had never experienced anything this devastating in his visions before. It was more than he could handle alone.

Three Dreams

Moments Before, One Hundred Fifty Miles West of the Hawaiian Islands

The Japanese cruise ship, Emperor, was in route to Osambashi in Yokahama, Japan under the command of a well-seasoned Captain, George Kieler. Built in the 60's, she was a an 800 foot long, 90 foot wide, 69,153 ton luxury liner that accommodated 1,828 passengers in her 915 luxury cabins, which, rivaled the best hotels on land. A swimming pool, beauty salon, theater, 3 restaurants, 5 elevators, spa, gymnasium, shopping center, and other amenities entertained the passengers during their cruise to Japan. She was now cruising at ten knots, in almost surreal calm waters. Couples strolled the promenade deck, unaware of the tragedy that would take the lives of the 1621 hands aboard. Two freak companion events were about to occur.

Below them, strange gravitational activity was tearing the ocean bottom apart. The sea floor rocked, then suddenly opened. One block of crust dropped below the other and sloped at 28 degrees, thereby displacing an immense amount of seawater. Movement under the ocean bed then produced an earthquake, which, in turn generated a tidal wave. A landslide in a nearby submarine canyon moved 8 billion metric tons of rocks.

The same quake opened the sea floor 140 miles Southwest of the *Emperor*, creating fissures, which swallowed the ocean itself, along with sea life and oceanic debris. The crust here would thrust up at 26 degrees. Two axes of spreading existed simultaneously.

The fissures closed as suddenly as they had opened, forcing tons of scalding water vertically to the surface, causing bores that would crest at 28 and 30 meters, a height never seen before. This caused the Mother of twin Tsunamis. Each Titan was approaching each other from opposite directions at 600 miles per hour, with outstretched arms that expanded 140 miles across.

The luxury liner's fate, this day, was to meet its destiny, with both.

When the concussion hit the ship, Captain Keiler jumped to his feet and ran for the bridge. He felt the deck shudder under his feet. Several passengers came running to the balcony rails to see what had happened, while others looked out from their outside view portholes.

"Where did that sound come from? Sounded like an explosion," he asked the first officer as he scanned the horizon.

"Dunno, Sir. Sounded like a cannon went off."

"Maybe it's a ship in trouble, trying to signal us. Any in the area?"

"No sir."

"Then what was it? It didn't come out of nowhere." Suddenly he remembered what he'd read about the Titanic. "Send up a flare, just in case." Although he tried to speak evenly, his voice quivered. The only time he ever experienced the ocean shuddering under his feet, was when he was aboard a battleship, off the coast of France. When the big guns fired on Normandy, it shook the whole ship. The vibration was the same. His mind raced. 'Maybe it's another island forming, just like the Hawaiian Islands have, over the millennia,' he thought. That old feeling of impending doom shot a red flag up in his brain, just like it did the day his ship sank in the English Channel. *Take it easy*, he told himself, 'this is not the same.'

"Radar. Have anything?"

"Yes sir, I'm getting something. I'm, I'm not sure what it is. Come look for yourself sir."

Captain Kieler turned, doubt still visible on his face, and began to move toward the radar screen. The seaman looked above the captain's head, eyes as wide as saucers. Terrified, he made the sign of the cross. "Jesus, Mary and Joseph.... Look captain, it must be over eighty feet high!"

All eyes turned in time to see the bore wave looming over them, blocking the sky.

"West-three-quarters-north," the captain shouted, in a futile effort to head into the surge.

The wave snatched the ship like a giant fist trying to catch a fly. The second Titanic wave slammed into the first, curling itself around the liner like a mother's blanket around a child. They piled up, adding another 20 meters to their height, then crashed into the sea, breaking her in half as if she were a matchstick. The sickening sound of people screaming, rails splintering, and tearing steel, drowned any order for a SOS that might have been sent. Thunderous rumbles of seams ripping open, and steel being snatched from its mountings out-screamed the cries of passengers and the order to abandon ship.

In a matter of seconds' cargo, furniture, fixtures and other debris tumbled out through the gaping hole in her stomach. Buoyant casks

Three Dreams

and crates that were belched out soared to the surface. An explosion flung an engine and other large objects some distance from the doomed liner. The ship was borne swiftly to its doom. In seconds she was sucked under, leaving belches of bubbles, debris, and passengers behind. Moments later people, and remnants of their lives, lay strewn across the dark dispassionate seabed below. Those who fought to survive soon gave up any hope of survival. The water was too cold, too deep, and too dispassionate.

Above, dead passengers floated among the debris of the disaster, while a lone airplane flew above, oblivious to the catastrophe below. All was eerily quiet…say for a tiny voice coming from below.

Chris's face turned white. He stood there with the phone against his ear, his mouth open. All along he strongly suspected Scott was gifted, saw things before they happened, but the reality of this prediction stunned him. He had never heard him predict anything outside of forthcoming earthquakes, but this time he was making it known he had *seen* the tidal waves and told him about it. He thought Scott was so scared, that he didn't realize what he was saying.

He quizzed him further. "What do you mean, tidal waves? Where? When?"

Without thinking Sky dropped the medallion into her pocket and moved toward Chris.

Phil and Sky could hear Scott screaming through the phone, even from where they stood. They quickly moved close to Chris's ear, to listen in.

"Two giant tidal waves…I think somewhere off the islands. Chris, there's a ship out there…it's going down. Cripes…." Terror clogged his throat.

Phil's forehead was corrugated, his whole manner subtly changed.

Alarmed, Phil grabbed the phone away from him, and put it to his ear. "What ship, man? What ship?" The chords in his neck stood out. His breathing quickened. By now he had forgotten all about the story. He had to know about the ship, the baby. He had come to believe them.

Chris snatched the phone back. "Can you see the name of the ship?"

Softly he breathed, "the *Emperor.* She's gone." There was a long pause. He was crying. "It's true Chris. It's true...I can hear the child. I know it. This is the ship we've been dreaming about."

"You say it's already happened?"

"It's too late. It's already gone down. I think it has...." He was sobbing now. "The child...I can see the child now. There's a birthmark on her leg...and...and the hands.... I can see them Chris, just like you said. She's really there. My God. We've got to get her. Chris, Chris...?" Phil could hear the anguish in his voice.

Chris snatched the phone from Phil. "Scott! Pull yourself together. Meet me at the office. I'm on my way. You hear me Scott? Leave now." His heart was punching through his chest.

He cradled the phone and looked at Phil, then to Sky, and then to back to Phil. "Now do you think it's made up? Believe us now? I admit I wasn't sure of any of this either, but now I am."

"Well, I'll be damned." Phil tucked his thumbs in the top of his pants and gave them a quick upward jerk.

"The baby. Did he say the baby had a birthmark on *her* thigh?" His emotions were like a bag of wild cats, fighting to get out. He didn't like the way his heart was pounding and his pulse was racing. He was impatient for an answer. An inner excitement began to glow.

"I think he said it was on her leg," Sky offered. "You saw it Chris. Where was it?" She didn't know why she asked; it really didn't matter, under the circumstances, where it was, she didn't believe it anyway.

Chris tried to recall where it was located. Seconds ticked off in his mind but he didn't rush. "I'm not sure...let me see...I think...I think, yes, it was on her left thigh." Not giving Phil's question any thought he went on to instruct Sky to call Steve on his cell phone and asked Phil to call Lou and Cuppy on the desk phone, to ask them to meet him at his office right away. "Tell them what Scott just told us."

"Right," says Phil. His daughter had a birthmark on her upper thigh. *No, it couldn't be. That's preposterous.* He tried to swallow. His mouth was dry. *It can't be her...could it? Reincarnation? Nah,* he told himself, but his heart was a little less heavy. A feeling of excitement that he hadn't experienced in a long while began to rise.

Each made their calls while Chris gathered some clothes for Sky and himself in an overnight bag. He knew it would be days before they'd return. He tossed down the rest of his beer and looked around to see if there was anything he missed.

"Hold up a second, I forgot something," said Sky as she disappeared through the bedroom door. A few moments later she returned empty handed.

"I thought you had to get something," Chris said.

"Couldn't find it. Doesn't matter. Let's go."

They left without locking the doors.

Roberta M. Alleman

4:10 p.m. June 5

They tried to leave as quietly as possible, but as soon as they heard the ignition turn over, the reporters came rushing toward the alley. Chris pushed the car in reverse and quickly backed out the driveway but the reporters caught up to the car before he could race away. Cameras flashed, reporters were yelling, while others shook their fist at Phil.

Stomping hard on the accelerator, tire rubber was laid down on the pavement as they surged forward. Reporters peppered countless questions at their retreating backs.

"Whew! They're going to be pissed at me. Oh well, they'll get over it." Phil said as he waved to his colleagues through the back window

"Chris. What are you going to do," says Sky.

He glanced at the rear view mirror. There was a bedlam of horn-tooting journalists piled up behind them. He pushed harder on the accelerator.

Everything was happening so fast. Sky wondered where this road would take them. Was there really a tidal wave? Did a ship go down? And what about this baby? She pulled down the vanity mirror and dug down into her purse for her makeup. Thinking it was too quiet; she reached over and flicked the radio on. Static. She searched for another station.

Chris felt her hand on his knee and covered it with his own and gave it a reassuring squeeze. He smiled to himself. Her hand of his knee and the racing of his heart brought his memory back to the mortifying day when he was twelve and Lorraine was thirteen and they were going to do "it" for the first time. The minute she placed her hand on his leg, he ejaculated. Embarrassed, he told her he had forgotten he had to do some chores before his dad got home and raced away. '*Poor Lorraine. I wonder if she ever figured it out,*' he wondered, semi amused. He would never let himself be alone with her after that.

"Chris...did you hear me," asks Sky. "What are you going to do?"

Three Dreams

"Don't know. Have to wait and see what pops up next." Looking through the rear view mirror he realized he had to pick up speed to stay ahead of the ensuing cars.

They watched the houses and shops slide by. The sultry air was alive with the chattering of customers and merchants. Islanders and tourists alike, who crowded the streets, were all looking for bargains?

Sky searched the radio for music. Suddenly it blared, *"...Tsunami was believed to have caused this phenomena. The Coast Guard and other rescue vessels are racing to the scene. The 'Emperor' was a luxury liner sailing to Japan with 1828 passengers and crew aboard. It was expected...."*

Chris turned it off.

Phil was thunder struck. He nodded absent-mindedly. He couldn't believe his ears. *It's true,* he thought. *It really did happen. My God...those poor bastards. They won't find anyone alive...they're all gone.* Tears welled up from a hidden place.

Silence fell over the car as it sped toward the Administration building.

Phil broke the quiet. "What is a tidal wave exactly," he asked, trying to control the emotion in his voice.

Chris glanced sideways at Sky and gave her hand a quick squeeze; as if to say, *go ahead honey, do your stuff.*

"I'm sure you've heard of the Ring of Fire, haven't you," Sky asked.

"Yeah. It's where there are fractures in the earth and huge plates from the fractures float on magma and they're constantly passing each other. It looks like a giant surgical scar and the rift circles the earth one and half times. Over time pressure builds. Occasionally, when one plate passes another, one of them rises. "They run along the coast of most countries...right?"

"Simply put, but yes. Japan has a trench 23,00 feet deed and is the sight of many major earthquakes. When there's an under sea eruption, tons of water are displaced and it generates a Tsunami, which can travel up to 600 miles or more per hour. They have the power of 1,000 hurricanes. There were eleven occurrences in the 1990's, which killed more than 4,000 people. In 1962 two and a half thousand people lost their lives in Chile, 61 in Hilo, and 150 people elsewhere...all from the same Tsunami. Many burn themselves out before they hit the coastlines, but the few that do reach land can devastate the coastal population. An Alaskan Tsunami can reach Hawaii in 6 hours, Chile in 15 hours," Sky responded.

"Also, there's not just one big wave with a Tsunami... They usually come in ten or more waves. Water is drawn up from harbors first, and then in comes the semi-large waves, then the larger, then the largest. They arrive 5 to 90 minutes apart," added Chris

"My God. What about this one? Didn't it happen in the middle of the ocean? How can that be? Shouldn't people be warned?"

"Yes, that is most unusual. We won't know until we get there. If people are to be warned, they will be. We're prepared for these things," Sky says.

Nothing else was said as they closed the distance between them and the Administration.

As they arrived, a frenzy of reporters rushed toward them. Flashbulbs exploded, cameras whirred. Furry mikes that looked like rats speared on a stick were shoved in their direction. Pressing forward, the reporter's questions were pointed and barbed. They were seeking the story of the century and were looking for blood to get it. In the commotion others hissed for them to be still. The lenses of their camera reflected the sunlight like a cowboy of old, standing on a mesa signaling the Calvary with a mirror, warning them of an impending Indian ambush.

The reporters, who sought a good position, pushed about administration guards. It was sheer pandemonium. The area buzzed with curiosity and speculation. With the whirring of photographer's motorized cameras, the throng of newspaper reporters with tape recorders and their boisterous camera crews, police, and the like, it reminded them of piranha at feeding time.

Soon several police cars pulled up with sirens blaring. Jostled officers ordered the reporters back to the curb. One uniformed guard stepped to the edge of the street, smiled apologetically, then motioned them into the employee's parking lot. In a minute or so there was enough room for their vehicle to ease through. Chris swept into his parking spot at the rear of the building. Quickly they jumped out and ran for the entrance. They hurriedly climbed the stairs, and then entered the fireproof door to the third floor where Paul's office was located.

As they entered Chris glanced around at the faces but ignored the sidelong looks from those colleagues who pretended to be busy. He

Three Dreams

went about his job; seemingly oblivious of other's questioning stares. Indeed, he was not.

Scott stood over his desk perusing a printout of the seismic activity over the past hour, while mumbling to himself. He had endured the whispering voices, the turning heads, and the questioning eyes when he arrived and was shaken by it. He was tempted to rush off to the nearest bar and was still seriously considering it when Chris arrived.

"What's the skinny," Chris asked as he looked over Scott's shoulder. He noticed he was trembling.

"I've never seen anything like it." His voice was shaky. Chris knew there was only a thread holding him together. "Look here. You can see the location of the two eruptions…one 47 minutes ago, the other 45 minutes. Look at those curves! Cripes! They're from seismic activity about 100 miles off of the Kaiwi Channel! It not only indicates an earthquake but," pointing to the irregularity of the graph line, "look here! There's a new rift approximately 80 miles South of it. Looks like the earthquake tore open the whole bottom along a currently unknown fault. Amazing! Just amazing. Never saw anything like it. Now look here. Nothing. It's like now you see us, now you don't. Its onset and secession only took minutes." He shoved the graphs in Chris's direction.

Chris fixed his eyes on the wave pattern of the Tsunamis. He hoped Scott would immerse himself in his work, to keep him from thinking about the *Emperor*. He always worked indefatigably, bringing perception and intelligence to his teammates. In spite of his drinking, his ability to predict earthquakes, his passion and enthusiasm were what kept him on the payroll.

He hoped keeping him busy would keep him from falling apart.

"Any other crafts in the area?"

"Dunno. They're checking. They're following up with the Coast Guard."

A large man stopped to tell him Paul wanted to see him as soon as he came in. Another colleague waved him over to orient him with several of the same graphs that Scott has just shown him, exhibiting the erratic lines depicting the quakes. Chris waved him off and pointed to the ones he was currently holding. "Got them."

The graphs looked like scribbles to Phil, but he knew what they meant.

A third man showed Chris several figures while he rattled off the latest pertinent information that was coming in.

Chris offered a few suggestions, waved Sky and Phil toward his desk, then started for Paul's office.

Sky led Phil over to Chris's desk. He skirted the flat desk heaped high with computer printouts, graphs, and catalogues, documents, journals and other sundries of papers, then sat down. Sitting in the corner was a framed picture of Sky with a red ribbon draped over the edge. Attached to the ribbon was a gold seal that read, *The World's Greatest.*

"And I thought my desk was bad…man oh man…lookey here."

"Really something, isn't it…but he really knows where everything is under there," says Sky as her eyes fell on the ribbon.

Sky smiled as she recalled the day they had gotten it. Several months ago, they made reservations for a dinner for a sunset cruise aboard the *America 11 Sunset Sail.* The two-hour cruise was the craft itself—a 1987 American Cup 12-m class contender. The sailing was smooth and romantic, while they dined on lobster tail and Caesar salad. Soft music played in the background. When a complimentary bottle of Champagne was delivered, it was tied with the red ribbon and that very seal. They toasted each other as they enjoyed the unobstructed view while sailing along the coast, under a blanket of stars, toward Diamond Head.

Later they walked leisurely hand in hand along the beach to Fisherman's Wharf where they giggled and laughed and fed each other smoked fish and French fries. They capped the night off at the *Row Bar.* Feeling wonderful, like two high school kids, they sang along with live reggae, danced, and laughed at the corny jokes told by amateur stand-up comics. They arrived home in the wee hours of the morning singing at the top of their lungs. That romantic evening was topped off with a pillow fight and two sensual hours of lovemaking.

That night was the first time she had told him she loved him. She blushed just thinking of that night and found she was aroused. She looked quickly at Phil to see if he was watching her. Luckily he wasn't. She let her mind drift back. *'We're going to do that again…soon,"* she promised herself.

Someone calling her from across the room, informing her Paul wanted to see her, immediately interrupted her thoughts.

Before joining them she made Phil a cup of coffee and told him to wait. She wasn't sure if he had heard her, as he was deeply engrossed in an article in one of the journals. She left without further word. As she crossed the room she glanced back and she saw him reach for the coffee mug without taking his eyes from the page.

The article began, *we have known about plate tectonics for only about 40 years…*

Sky turned and looked toward Paul's office. Through the glass walls she could see Scott, Paul and Chris in a heated argument. Smiling, she slowly walked toward them. They reminded her of the Keystone Cops of the silent movies. Everyone was talking at the same time. In their vigor to get their point across, they flailed their arms about, making them appear animated.

By the time she reached the door she had stifled her laughter and felt sufficiently composed to enter. Hesitating at the door, she drew a deep breath, let out her last giggle, and then entered.

"Okay to come in?"

The phone rang, but neither she nor the ringing was heard over the din. Smiling to herself, she stood watching them. After waiting patiently for them to notice her she whistled and yelled, "Gentlemen! Gentlemen. Please. Can we have some semblance of order here? We're not going to get anywhere screaming at each other!"

All conversation ceased. The phone continued ringing.

"We can't accomplish anything with everyone talking at once. We have a crisis before us. Let's work together in finding some answers," she added.

Just then Cuppy and Lou burst through the door. Both were very excited. The phone stopped ringing.

"Do you believe it? Do you believe it," Cuppy says, pounding his fist on the desk. "I knew it. I just knew it. Didn't I tell you Lou? I just knew it." He seemed pleased with himself and beamed with as much pride as a man who just won a new Jaguar. "Okay, we're ready. When do we get started?"

"Hold your horses," says Paul. "First we need to get a hold of Search and Rescue. I hear they've already got three helicopters out there looking for survivors. Their cutter is on its way as well. The Air Force has sent some helicopters as well as the army. We'll have to wait until there some contact made. They'll contact us as to where the *Emperor* is located as soon as they find out."

"Already done," says Lou, holding up a chart. He quickly moved to the desk and pushed books and papers aside. He placed his finger on an empty spot in the Pacific where she was known to have gone down.

"And where did you get this exclusive information might I ask," says Paul.

"Connections," says Cuppy, winking.

The phone began to ring again.

Looking at the map, Sky could see it was only inches from the main island of Hawaii, but knew, in reality, it was perhaps 200 miles or more. "Was there any word of survivors," she asked, dreading what she may hear.

"Not yet," says Lou quietly.

"Have you seen those figures out there? They're the highest I've ever seen. If the *Emperor* was there, believe me, there will be no survivors. None," Scott says.

Sadness came over Paul's eyes. He stared off as if he were visualizing some unseen memory.

The phone continued ringing. Paul quickly composed himself, then grabbed the receiver and held it to his ear. He listened for a moment then extended it to Cuppy. "For you."

"Cuppy here." As he listened, all eyes were riveted on him. His face emanated a diversity of emotions in such a way that everyone could feel them. Solemnly he hung up the receiver. "That was the Coast Guard," he said, breaking the frozen mood. "It's confirmed. The *Emperor* is down. Search and rescue sighted the oil slick, and saw their air bubbles rising and spreading over the area. So far, there have been no survivors sighted. A lifeboat bearing their name was found floating upside-down with half its side ripped off…the only wood, it seems, that will mark their graves," he said in sad resignation. "They dropped a buoy at the sight. Tears welled in his eyes but he refused to give them up.

"Oh shit," said Lou softly.

A shudder ran around the room. Faces were grim. All were riveted to where they stood. Their colleagues, sensing the news, moved toward Paul's office. From the look on the faces within, they knew the outcome.

The news hit Chris like a sledgehammer. He felt penitence because he was privy beforehand in knowing the *Emperor's* fate.

Three Dreams

'*These are real people who died today, on a real ship,*' he thought. Before now, it wasn't real for him. Until now it was just a dream. Releasing his emotions, he slammed both fists on the desk, startling everyone. "Shit!"

"My God, all those people," Sky said softly. "Those poor, poor people." Her hand covered her mouth as if to stifle a cry. Her eyes clouded over with the sudden threat of tears. Disconcerted thoughts again ran through her mind. *Could it be true after all? Could this all be a coincidence? It has to be.*

"Are they sure there's no survivors…not anyone…anyone at all," Paul asked Cuppy, hopefully.

Words were unnecessary: the same thought came inevitably to the mind of everyone in the room.

Paul read the truth in his eyes, but did not want to grasp the horror of it all. He slumped like a discarded puppet into the nearest chair and tried to clear his head. He felt miserable and certain he'd never feel well again.

Chris sat down, sullen, feeling like two people.

The tenure of their mission had changed, for all of them.

News of the sinking flashed across the world. **THE WORST SEA DISASTER SINCE THE SINKING OF THE TITANIC,** the EXTRA edition reported. Headlines exploded in black ink: **1828 SOULS LOST AT SEA. POSSIBLE LONE SURVIVOR IN SINKING**. Above the leading story of one newspaper, the headline simply read, **PRAY!**

Also reported on the front page were the dreams of the three men and their prediction that a child would be found, miraculously, still alive within the hull. "Could this be the very ship that holds that tiny child in its death grip," they dramatically questioned.

And so, through radio, television, telephone, and word of mouth, the inexplicable, yet wonderful news traveled from continent to continent within hours, like ripples on water, in ever-ending circles.

Everyone was talking…in English, French, Spanish, Greek, Chinese, and Italian.

"You hear? I don't believe that rot. A hoax if you ask me! How could anyone survive anything like that?"

"It's a miracle. Blessed by God. They were chosen.…"

Discontented murmuring followed. "Nah! They're crackpots. They ought ta be shot for stirrin' people up."

"It's a miracle."

Much to the eye-rolling exasperation of scoffing of some, many believed there was a child and it could be saved…or they **wanted** to believe.

"I think it's wonderful. That child's probably crying for its momma right now."

Everywhere, onlookers whispered fervently among themselves. Rumors ran rampant. It was all people could talk about. Some said they were crazy, some believed there was a possibility of someone surviving, and some awaited the outcome while others prayed for the survival of the child, if there was a child. Regardless, all eyes were on Hawaii. As they watched and waited, they hoped for a miracle, just as Phil had. If once, just one incredulous miracle did take place, then life might be worth living just a little bit more. It would prove to them that their God had not deserted them after all. Sparing the life of this child would be a sign. Just the slightest possibility that there may be some substance to what the media was reporting, made them want to be a part of something wonderful.

Three Dreams

MEANWHILE

Paul stood in front of a large chart of the Pacific Ocean patiently waiting for his team of specialists to arrive. He hoped their accumulated experience might help him find the answers to questions the public would now be asking. His expression was decidedly unhappy.

A quiet assurance emanated from this gentleman. No one knew that own son-in-law was a passenger aboard that ship. Only this morning he and his daughter were waving him good-bye at the dock. He was grateful his wife, if she had to become ill, did so at this time. If she had not, their daughter would have accompanied him. She postponed he trip for another week. He felt guilty that he was glad she was not among the missing passengers. He could not picture his life without her.

"Ladies and Gentlemen…may I have your attention! I'm sure you all know of the recent events that have taken place, which caused this tragedy. Our figures indicate a triple phenomenon, unlike what has ever been experienced in the known history of man. The first massive magnitude that registered at Mw 8.7 took place here." He snapped the pointer on the page as if he were killing a fly.

"The second temblor, here at M7.4…and the landslide here…in-between. As you can see…" his voice broke. Composing himself, he went on. "As you can see, the intensity of the seismically is located within a comparatively small area. Our guess is that the tectonic action caused these rifts to open and close so quickly, perhaps in only minutes, that in all probably they caused these titanic tidal waves. When they moved toward each other and overcame the *Emperor*, they, in essence, canceled each other out. These Cyclops, we believe, may have crested at 150 feet, when they met each other head-on. The *Emperor* had no place to go…but down. We rightfully speculated that these waves negated each other upon their impact because of the force that they produced. Running headlong into each other would be the only thing on this earth that could have stopped them. If this had not occurred, as horrible as it was, it would have wiped out populations from Alaska to the South Pole."

"So far 58 vigorous aftershock sequences have occurred with many more expected. The aftershocks will probably be felt for years. There's extensive flooding and earth movement reported along coastlines from Alaska, Japan, northeastern India, and the West Coast of North and South America. We can only imagine the devastation that would have left behind if these two giants headed landward...and thank God that it didn't."

"But Paul, there's no rift out there...or at least none that's been recorded. Where did it come from...and in two places yet," a voice interrupted with a touch of impatience.

"Mother earth is a living, breathing entity. She's always changing her makeup. We can never be sure where and when she will decide to pull a phenomenal episode, such as this, out of her cap again. You imagine there's a great deal about the ocean bottom we haven't been privy to yet. It's obvious there's a new rift out there we weren't aware of. We have to rethink plate boundaries now...that's what we're paid for." As he spoke, he allowed his eyes to dart from one face to another. "Investigations, research, data, and all other investigative tools are like onions, whose layers have to be peeled away. That could take years, or even centuries. We'll just have to do more research to see what we come up with. We don't have all the facts yet. It's my guess this was one big hell of a plate that the liner unluckily was sailing across when the whole damn thing decided to shift. The shift caused a giant avalanche in one of the canyons, which displaced billions of tons of rock. This only added to the disaster. Again, it's up to us to dig up the answers. Now everybody get their act together and let's act like professionals. There's reporters out there but you aren't take give them any information. Understand? Nothing. That's my job. Now let's get back to work."

Theories were discussed, and rejected over the next hour while Paul prepared to go outside to give a press release. He dreaded it because he knew it was his sad duty to bring this horror into sharp believable focus for the loved ones of the passengers who went down.

On his way out he passed Chris. "Chris, Scott, got a minute?" He stopped and leaned against the wall, propping one foot against it.

"Ya Paul, what is it," says Chris.

"I'm not gonna ask you guys if these stories are true. I've got troubles of my own right now, but I want to know if they're true. The radio in my office stays on most of the time so I couldn't miss

Three Dreams

it...about you guys. It's on every station, no one can. I don't need your problems too...and ah...from what they're saying, it's a shit load." He paused for a few moments and appeared to be thinking of a way to say what he had on his mind. "Tell me this, do you think there may be more survivors? I mean...it was a big ship...somebody could have...."

"As far as we know Paul, there's no one else, if indeed, there is a survivor at all."

Paul sighed and let his shoulders slump. He thought, *my poor darling Kate. How is she going to take the news that she's a widow now? How am I going to tell her? And mom...as sick as she...this didn't need to happen now.*

"Okay guy, thanks. I can't just go out and tell those families there's no hope. Christ, there are brothers and sister, mothers and fathers, and children...children that are lost." His mood looked understandably dark.

As they started away, Paul called to them, "It's just...just that my son-in-law was...was aboard that ship. I thought...."

Before they could respond, he was gone.

There was a bank of television reporters waiting outside...all looking for a 'Q' rating. Paul ignored any and all questions about the dreams and the child. He went through everything else chronologically, objectively, and quickly without rushing, leaving out speculations and theories.

If there was is survivor, maybe there could be two, he kept thinking. *Perhaps my son-in-law might be out there alive. Maybe they're already rescuing him. Maybe there are others. Impossible! There's no one alive down there.* Still he held desperately on to that hope.

Just as Chris dispersed the team, his beeper began pulsating. He knew it was either Steve or Dr. Isu.

Cuppy rushed over when he saw him checking the number of the caller. Lou followed close behind.

"Is that Dr. Isu," Cuppy asked.

"Either him or Steve."

He walked over to his desk and dialed the number. It was only when the phone at the other end rang that he realized who had called. It was Steve.

"Heard the news?"

"Which news," he asked cynically.

"Turn on your set man. The wire service has already picked it up. You guys are all over the TV. Destiny has played you a dirty hands my man. I suppose you heard about my secretary." He was quiet for a moment. Chris guessed he was trying to gather the words to make light of the theft. "I can't tell you how very sorry I am Chris. You know I wouldn't betray you buddy. I'll make it up to you I swear I will. Goddamn her. She'd better hide, and hide well. If I ever find her I'll...." There was a long pause. "Regardless, it's a human interest story now and the media is out to get their lion's share. They're not sure whether your devils or angels, but they're going to play it to the hilt. I'm sorry man, what can I say? What can I do to make it up to you?"

"Nothing. It can't be undone...and yes, I got the word about your secretary. Where did you dig her up from?"

"That bitch. That Goddamn bitch. I wanted to tell you myself. I wish I could tell you how very sorry I am," he repeated with remorse, wondering if things would ever be the same between them. There was another long pause. "Wait a minute, Dr. Isu wants to speak with you."

"Hello Mr. Healy. I'm sure you've heard. Don't be too hard on Steve. There's no way he could have known."

"Unfortunately I have. No matter about the theft, why does the man upstairs let things like this happen? Over 1600 people snuffed out. Why didn't the dreams tell me more about them?"

"Perhaps God allows such thing to happen so that you may open eyes that were previously closed. Sometimes something good comes out of disaster. Fate is not immune to our efforts to change it."

"What good can come out of loss all those lives?"

"We may not see in the beginning, but miracles do happen...many where we least expect them. Take your vision for instance. Certainly she had some objective in her visitation. Listen to the soul...the voice within. If you listen carefully, you get to hear everything you didn't want to hear in the first place. When doubt arises, defeat is not far behind. Kind sir, we are positioned, not by chance, but design, within the context of those other lives we may touch. The gift obligates us to contribute our best efforts. Take some quiet time and listen...see. The answers will come. Trust the soul. Trust yourself. All of your life you've followed the rules of cause and effect. If you turn on the faucet, water runs out. If you drop a glass to the floor, it breaks. We know what to expect when these things happen…we 'see the future,' as it were. Then again, the glass may not break when it drops to the floor. You will not know what will happen absolutely until it occurs."

"So what you're saying is that if I do go, and if there is a child and the rescue is successful, I may never know for sure that it was my actions that changed the course of the event."

"Because you do not have the answers to all of your questions now does not mean answers will not come. In my investigations of the paranormal, I have learned that one-size-fits-all is not applicable. The purpose, meaning, content, and the subjects all vary. We believe, in your case, that the source originated in another intelligence, intelligence with some emotional connection. This cannot be ignored."

"But I told you, I don't know who the hell she is."

Ignoring his comment the doctor went on. "The *Sea Star* was conducting their underwater archeology 90 miles from the *Emperor* when she went down and in their spirit to cooperate they have volunteered their craft and equipment in the search and rescue. We are to meet them at the site."

"Who are we? You mean me? Not on your life! You guys can take it from here. You already know what's going to happen."

Chris not wanting to go to the site? Lou and Cuppy stared at each other blankly, mouths agape. They couldn't believe their ears. Their mouths were merely a grave for their tongues.

Concerned for Chris's state of mind Dr Isu asked, "Exactly what is it you're afraid of Chris? That you won't come back? Is it fear of disbelief, of ridicule, or being ostracized from your profession? Or is it that there is no such child, but only metal rubbing against metal? What is it?" Pause. "We can't choose our feelings. From time to time we'll be swept away by feelings we don't choose, but we can choose our actions. Whoever reached out to touch you men selected each of you for a purpose…a specific purpose. However, by touching you, she has touched all of us. We can only speculate why that is. You know, within you, that you must go. There is no other way or the dream will not be fulfilled."

"How do you figure that Doctor?"

"Think about it. So far everything you've dreamed has come to pass. Is that a coincidence? Certainly not! You know in your heart that this is the ship. There was no indication in your dream when the ship would sink, only that it would sink and that you would rescue the child. No one else can do it. That is why these two other men were not allowed entrance. It was not to be. You must be there. The outcome can't be predicted if you don't. Perhaps the child will die."

His comment unnerved Chris. "Doc, even you can't tell me this is the ship and that there is a child alive within." He did not tell the doctor what Scott has relayed to him. Maybe he needed more reassurance. Maybe he needed someone to tell him that this was just some crazy joke. "How do we know this is the one? Aren't dreams supposed to be symbolic of something else?" His brows drew together in a troubled frown.

"You know. You already know it within your soul. Search for the answers there. Cuppy and Lou have readied a boat for us in anticipation of this event. They began preparing months ago. He believed in you…and the dreams…and so do we. We'll meet you at the dock in one hour. Scott reported to you what he saw. Now we must act."

Chris was caught off guard. *How did he know about Scott's vision? Did he call him and tell him? He had to or how else would he have known?* Before he had a chance to refuse he had hung up. Deep down, he knew that what he was saying was true. He wondered why he was so reluctant to admit that he wanted to wholeheartedly believe the dreams. A part of him just wouldn't permit that.

He sat down to gather his thoughts…to look into his soul, as Dr. Isu put it. There was something in the way he spoke to him, that gave him the impression he knew something he didn't. It gave him the willies, like the doctor already knew what the outcome would be. Could it be true? Does he have some sort of clairvoyance like Scott?

Without warning the vision of the woman appeared before him again. She reminded him of his mother, after she had taken her bath. Her auburn hair would be stuck to her neck and face in the same way, until she towel-dried it. Dewdrops of moisture covered the woman's skin. Her saturated clothes clung to her body. He could see a ship lying on the seabed behind her.

Clearly she said, "The time has come."

He jerked his head in the direction of the words. "But why me," he asked aloud. She did not answer. Her image faded, leaving him only with the name of the silent ship behind her. He sat there for a few moments staring at it, not quite grasping what was before him.

Then it dawned on him. She was leaving him a message…a clue. He bolted upright when he realized she was showing him the name of the ship. **It was the *Emperor*.**

Sky, Lou, Scott, and Cuppy had heard him, seemingly, talking to thin air. They approached and looked at him with worried eyes.

Others around him also sensed something was going on. During the vision he appeared to be looking at someone or something, but nothing was there. Those nearby heard him ask, "why me," but couldn't see anyone. Most of them had already heard about the dreams from the TV and didn't know what to think. Most thought Chris was too bright to set himself up for ridicule with ridiculous stories. Many dismissed it as being overworked, while his true friends voiced, "If he says it's true, then it's true." They did not question it and were ready to defend their friend against anyone who said otherwise.

"I just saw it…the *Emperor*," he said as he reached for Sky's arm. "She was showing me. It is the *Emperor*!" All doubt left his face. A river of emotions erupted. Until that moment he had never put any real credence in the dreams. The reality of the unreality jolted him into action.

"Okay, come on, let's go. Where's that boat you were talking about?" he said with a voice that concealed the urgency he felt. Or so he thought. Despite the tension, he was amazed at how good he felt.

He grabbed his jacket and headed for the door. Lou, Sky, Scott and Cuppy were on his heels.

Cuppy yelled, "This way."

They emerged into the painfully bright sunlight and dashed for the van that was already waiting in the lot. Chris made a slight detour to retrieve his black bag from his car. Waiting for them outside the gate was more media vehicles, onlookers, and a sundry of reporters that represented principal papers and TV stations of the country. Cameras were again shoved in their faces as they approached the street. Correspondents and journalists were all interrogating at the same time.

"No comment. No comment," Chris said through closed windows.

Once in he looked around for Phil, but couldn't locate him in the crowd. He sped toward Pearl Harbor.

The wide road followed the natural curve of the coast. As they pulled into the marina they passed open-air restaurants, boutiques, bait shops, hotels, and other tourist attractions. While looking for a parking slot Cuppy pointed to a diving barge, which was moored at the dock. The 'barge' was a cross between Noah's ark and a PT109. What looked like a mast held various wet suits, tanks, fishing gear and various sized ropes. It was painted a battleship gray while the words *Blue Pelican* painted on its side, were in yellow. Various accoutrements such as tanks, tarps, boxes, wet suits, ropes, rain gear, and much more, littered the deck. Cuppy had worked his wizardry once again.

Looking around, Chris couldn't help but wonder where Cuppy had dug up this tub from.

6:55 p.m. June 5

As they boarded Cuppy asked triumphantly, "Well, what do you think," then said quickly, in a foreboding tone, "We've got trouble. A storm is coming in." He tilted his head and looked askew at them, as if it were his fault. Chris looked out to the skyline. Although the day was warm and windy, it was the kind that tricks one into thinking all was well with the world-if you didn't know a storm was fast approaching.

Doctors' Malik and Isu boarded next, carrying several boxes containing instruments and equipment. It was their intent to continue monitoring the three men to the completion of the rescue and beyond. Behind them were their entourage…two assistants.

"This craft looks rigorous enough," says Dr. Malik. Eyeing the supplies on deck she asked, "Have everything you need?"

Dr. Isu looked like he wanted to run to the safety of the dock, but said nothing. He was not used to such "clutter."

Cuppy lovingly ran his hand over the weathered wooden rail as if he were caressing a mink stole. "Yes ma'am, we do. The boat's antiquated but reliable. She was built in Italy, weighs 11924 tons and propels with diesel. Came into service in 1967. Yup, she did…1967. Take you anywhere you want to go," he said proudly. "Your colleagues are already setting up shop below with the instruments you sent over yesterday."

Yesterday? How could they have known yesterday, Chris wondered.

Cuppy turned to the men on deck. He described who they were and what role they would play in the rescue. "The Recompression chamber operator Mr. Jim Thorpe." He was about forty-five, long cheeked, lean, brown-haired, a constant excitement glinting in his deep-set blue eyes. "Stand by diver, Joe Darden." Joe, who was a six-foot, broad-shouldered bass-voiced man of about 40, flashed him a gap-toothed smile as he shook his hand. "Second diver, Mr. Ron 'Pappy' Daniel.' Ron, a black man, was in his late thirties with eyebrows that were bushy and black, a startling incongruity to his snow-white hair. Chris supposed he received his nickname for that very reason. "Here's Ray Chaney, our radio operator." Ray was about

5'6" tall with a round face and a belly to match. He smiled at him through a bushy mustache. "Our doctor, Doc Henry." He didn't look like a doctor with his greasy shorts, torn T-shirt and a four-day growth on his chin. "He'll keep you alive. They're all old diving allies. This here is Nate, our dive coordinator, and this here is D.C. They're going to get us there and back in one piece. Nothing but the best. Had more volunteers, but couldn't take 'em all. You all know Lou, of course."

"Right here is your diving gear. Although Chris could dive to 160 feet with two 100 tanks, his time down would be too short so I got the Superlite 176b's. Easier to use, longer time below."

"Just to be safe," he continued, "I've thrown in a pony bottle. It holds enough oxygen to get a man out of trouble if something goes wrong with his tanks." He knew it wouldn't help much at the depth Chris would have to go to get him to the top, but it might come in handy in an emergency. "We have pure oxygen, Heli-ox and SUR do2. Take your pick. And here are the groceries. Can't go anywhere without them. Gotta eat," he said as he nudged Lou in the ribs.

Everyone's eyes were glued to the frozen TV dinners, which, they hoped they wouldn't get hungry enough to have to eat.

"Where'd you get the 160 feet from," asked Chris.

"Where else? I've been listening to the Coast Guard's transmissions. That's how deep she lies. The *Sea Star* is maybe less then 30 minutes from the sight right now so we'd better get going."

Secretly the *Blue Pelican* had already loaded a tiny decompression chamber, which was an elliptical hermetically sealed thick glass tank made especially for the child. Together, Lou and Cuppy had examined every problem they encountered, stripping it bear to examine every pitfall. The sheer scale of the project captured their imaginations. After many hours of work they could see the possibilities in that it could save the child's life. Final decisions were irrevocable. It had to work.

The receptacle was an adaptation of an earlier invention Lou had been laboring over but had not been created for human beings. It was constructed to recover live specimens from the depths of the oceans. The two-foot chamber was conspicuously absent of the air compressor, which would normally be coupled to it. With the precision of a surgeon Lou devised a way to enable the air inside the see-through tank to build up equal pressure of that below, without attachments. Lou and Cuppy had begun working secretly in anticipation of the day it would be needed. Lou reasoned the compression hose could not wind through the wreck and scaled down necessary parts that would be attached to the underside of the carrying case. There were too many jagged edges below. It couldn't be risked. They worked day and night creating this tiny see-through cradle that would sustain the life of the child as Chris ascended to the top. Warmth, oxygen, pressurization, weight and strength were only a few considerations taken in its care and completion. A guinea pig from the pet store lived up to its name as they tested the apparatus. It survived with no ill effects. They believed it would work.

Earlier, Phil had left the *National Oceanic and Atmospheric Administration* and had taken a cab to the harbor. On the way he made several phone calls via his cell phone. One was to his editor, one to a TV station, and one to a friend who owned a racing yacht. If all went well, his friend would be ready to leave at a moment's notice and they could follow the *Blue Pelican* to the site. He wanted full visual and audio reporting of the unfolding events to be broadcast throughout the world. He was excited about the possibility of taking viewers directly to the scene of headline news being made.

Realizing he needed a closer proximity to the unfolding events, Phil called the manager of the local TV station whom he had known for years. He promised him the story of a lifetime if he'd commit to letting him have a mobile camera, a cameraman, a technician, sound man and other necessary equipment to telecast live, an ongoing, onboard, narrative broadcast. The magnitude of the disaster was still unknown but he assured him that his station would be the first on sight to report the extraordinary drama to the world, and first in getting the scoop. He agreed.

When he arrived, his wiry friend was already awaiting him. He was dressed in brown shorts, a T-shirt with *Zorro* written in red on the front, a red cotton zipper jacket, white sneakers and socks, and a blue cap with the word *Captain* embroidered on it. He waved Phil over the dock where his boat was moored.

Martin Lewis, age 63, was a colorful character who had participated in the 630 mile race from Sydney, Australia to Hobart, Tasmania, the Whitbread Round the World race, the America's Cup, and the Admiral's Cup races in the same sailboat. Two of those races encountered severe storms, and both times, he came through. He loved the element of danger. He not only feared the sea, but also was fascinated by it.

"How exciting," he said as they shook hands. "I wouldn't have missed this for the world. I may not have to travel so far, but this sounds just as exciting as a world cup race."

"I have someone coming over with equipment I'll need to broadcast out there. We'll have to wait for him. He'd better get here quick," he said impatiently, tapping his fingers on his thigh. He knew it would be getting dark in a few hours. "How about the *Blue Pelican*? Know where she is? Has she left yet?"

"Look over to your left…two docks down. What do you see?"

Phil craned his neck to see above the other boats that were creaking in their moorings between the two docks. He located her by the mock crow's nest the crew had erected five years ago. "Great. They haven't left yet. Good…good. I hope they don't sail before those guys get here."

Within 40 minutes everything he asked for had arrived, along with two newscasters from the 6:00 o'clock news.

"Just a little insurance from the top man," retorted one as he and the crew boarded.

Forty-five minutes later both boats had slipped their moorings and slid from the harbor.

7:41 p.m. June 5

As soon as they were underway, everyone aboard the Blue Pelican seated themselves in chairs grouped around the old chart table. Cuppy had anticipated information they would probably request and had the ship plans already lain out on the table. Since there wasn't enough room for everyone to be seated, the remainder leaned over shoulders for a view of the plans. As they were being studied, discussions elevated as to where the child might be located and the best route to get there. Each and all had an idea on how to conduct the search.

As they exchanged ideas, Scott continued to go over the plans. His mind, which sorted and reviewed the data, was *reading in pictures.* He ran his eyes over every square inch of the page, but his censors couldn't detect anything. He scanned again. This time they fell on the infirmary. He then leaned back, pressed three fingers to his lips and smiled.

"Remember the *Titanic,*" D.C. asked. "Everyone ran up...up toward the stern. Her bow was underwater. They had to go up. I'd say, the stern."

"We don't think the *Emperor* sank that slowly," said Dr. Isu. "No one had time to run anywhere."

"What about the dining room? Is that a possibility," someone asked.

It was a suggestion, which satisfied no one.

"It's up for grabs. We just don't know. She could be anywhere," says Lou.

"I think we've also forgotten that the ship is probably strewn all over the sea bed," added Sky cynically, "maybe she's there on the sea bed."

Chris shot her a stern look.

"How about her cabin? Wouldn't the mother be caring for her new born in her cabin," asked Dr. Malik.

"That's a good possibility," a voice replied.

"What about the infirmary? Maybe she just had the child and was still under her doctor's care."

"There's another good possibility and one I like better," said Cuppy. "At least we know where the sick bay is. We don't have any idea where her cabin was."

"Do we have a manifest of the passengers?"

Cuppy winked. "I do believe we do." He reached into a folder and pulled out the list of names. "I knew you'd ask for them," he grinned.

"If we cross off all of the men and all of the crew, we may be able to cut the list down somewhat. I believe she was an American, so we can also cross off any really unusual names like Wong and so on. Another thing. See where there is a 'C' next to some of the names, cross those off too. That indicates the passenger is a child."

"She's..." Scott interjected.

"The 'H' placed next to the names mean they're handicapped, so that cuts the list down even more," interrupted Lou.

After eliminating these names the list had dropped to 678. Not good odds.

Scott's jaw muscles rippled as he moved impatiently beside Chris. Not daring to interrupt him, he waited miserably, drumming his fingers on the table. Finally he pushed back his chair and rose.

"God-damn-it, would you people listen," he said in a loud voice. All eyes turned to Scott, who was learning to curse his newly emerged status as resident clairvoyant. There was a period of stillness before he continued. He gazed around the room and, satisfied that all attention was on him says, "The child is in the infirmary...sick bay, or hospital, as some of you know it. You can find her there. We don't have much time." As he spoke he thumped a fastidious finger on the manifest.

Scott looked away, blinking rapidly. Surprisingly, no one challenged his statement. They were convinced he knew. All conversation ceased as to where she could be located and focused on how to rescue her.

There was an awkward moment when Pappy asked, "How are we supposed to bring the child up...if there is a child, that is," Stillness again. "We have no proof it's down there...and besides, if there is, and I doubt it, how are we supposed to get it to the top? Have you thought of that?"

Lou rose, excused himself, and then left the cabin. A minute or two later he returned carrying the chamber he devised that would bring the child safely to the surface.

"This is what we'll use. It's lighter than a jawbone of an ass so Chris won't split a gizzard carrying it and it's powered by its own small radioisotope source. Through the dreams, we think that there is at least a foot or two of air left in the cabin. The child can be placed into this chamber and be brought to the surface unharmed if," he hesitated again, "if she can be brought up in eighteen minutes." He pointed to a small cylinder attached to the bottom of the case; "This pony has been modified to hold eighteen minutes of pure oxygen. Whoever brings the child up will only have eighteen minutes, no more."

"It's damn cold down there, she'll freeze before she gets to the top, if she hasn't already," says Lucky. "What am I saying…there's no proof there is a living person down there. Three people dreaming about it don't make it true. We're just going on a wing and a prayer. Where's the hard proof?"

There was a guff laugh from behind him.

Dr. Isu, who had been listening quietly said, "No, we don't have proof, however, the sinking of this ship was dreamed about and that's true." His emotionless gaze settled on Lucky. "No one can dispute that. The tsunamis were dreamed about and that is also true. Why wouldn't we believe that there is a child? A civilized man would have to go see. He would not be able to escape it." He could not help smiling to himself. *These disbeliveers,* he thought. "If you did not believe, then why did you come along?"

Lucky nervously directed his gaze away from the doctor and focused on the small sliver of wood he worried over at the edge of the table. Long seconds passed. Then, clearing his throat he said, "I dunno. I thought…well…if there was a chance…I wouldn't let no baby die. I'd have ta help save it."

Dr. Isu nodded triumphantly. His stern expression dissolved and he smiled. *I knew it.* He walked over and patted him on the back. "The child is there, you'll see."

"We'll be contacting the *Sea Star* soon. She should have more information by the time we get there," says Cuppy.

After much discussion and pooling their efforts the group finally worked out a plan.

Each diver was given a water resistant black crayon. "X out each cabin you already checked so we don't double search. It'll tell us where you've been and where to find you if you get into trouble,"

Pappy instructed. "If the child isn't in sick bay, then we'll have to check them one by one. Might get pretty gruesome down there. Think you can handle it?" No one replied. "Well then, I suggest we get prepared."

Ominous clouds were gathering overhead.

A quarter hour later the men began preparing their equipment for the dive. Almost everything was ready and on stand-by. Cuppy had to seen to that. He had called in a lot of favors weeks before and was prepared with any type of equipment that may be needed. The team tied everything down in preparation of the oncoming storm.

After the meeting Chris sat down against a pile of ropes that were coiled on deck. His eyes fell upon an old golden box that had tarnished with age, laying a few feet away. His mind drifted to the one he treasured as a child. He kept only the most important and cherished items in this, and hid the key on a string around his neck. He smiled as he recalled these treasures; a dried frog he had found in the road, a yellow marble he called Jake, a frayed yo-yo string, two soda bottle caps and a broken jack-knife he had swapped for his hand-me-down belt.

With eyes closed and his face lifted to the sky he listened to the drone of the engines and the cadence of the ocean. This relaxed him and he was soon asleep. He found himself back on the farm where he was raised. He was about four years old then. He saw his parents were crying and they were holding each other.

"There's nothing we can do mamma. We have to let her go."

"Oh Hal, I just can't. She's my baby," his mother sobbed.

"We have to do what is best for the child. She'll be with you sister. She can't have any children and they love her. You know that," he said softly.

Chris' eyes fell on the bassinet near the old couch. He could see tiny hands pop over the top every so often. He knew it was his baby sister. She was born with red fuzz on her head a few weeks earlier. He had waited many times, with his ear pressed against his mother's stomach, for the little kicks that would come from within. He would squeal with laughter and run to tell daddy about it. His father would always say, "That's wonderful, now it's time for bed son." He'd then swoop Chris into his big arms and carry him upstairs. All of the children slept in one barracks-like room; the girls' side divided by a blanket hanging from two nails.

Three Dreams

It was more than 35 years ago but the image of his parents played out in his thoughts as if he were watching a movie.

He didn't stay in bed this night. He crept downstairs and hid behind the door to the living room...and listened. "You know your sister will take care of her. We've already talked this over with them and they promised to bring her back if they couldn't manage. They're waiting outside. We just can't afford another child right now mother. Think of the baby. What kind of life would she have here? We can't give her nuthin'."

"I just can't do it. It's like I'm abandoning her," his mother said, crying softly into her apron.

"We're not abandoning her mother. We're placing her in a loving home."

Chris was scared and ran from his hiding place. "What's the matter mommy?"

His mother scooped him up in her arms and held him tightly. "Take her. No...wait. I want to give her something. She put Chris down and walked hurriedly over to the kitchen drawer, which held her bible. She removed a small tin box. She removed a medal on a golden chain. "Give Patty this medal. It belonged to my dad. He had my initials engraved on the back before he gave it to me. I want her to have it when she's old enough. Chris looked at the medal. It had the same picture of Saint Elmo stamped on one side. As it turned on the end of the chain he could see something written on it but he was too young to read.

He watched as his dad sadly removed the wooden box containing the baby's clothes from the house, then the bassinet that held his tiny sister. He was never to see his sister again.

After the car drove away, his mother fled upstairs. His father slid to the floor and sobbed. That was to be the first and last time he would ever see his father shed a tear. He tried to comfort him, not really understanding what had happened.

He could not understand, that birth control was not known then, and that with a large family, failed crops and no money, people had to make some hard decisions. It was not that uncommon to give one or more of the children of a large family to relatives or friends to raise.

Chris snapped awake. He almost grinned to himself. His heart was beating fast. He tried to swallow but his mouth was dry.

"Of course!" The answer hit his conscious mind as he spoke those words. Everything fell into place. He remembered after his sister had gone her name was never brought up again. To do so would reduce his mother to tears and his father to anger. His Uncle Duke and Aunt Louise moved to Springfield a few weeks later. An occasional phone call came after they left. Later, a letter or two, then nothing. He had forgotten he had had a younger sister after a few months.

He sat there digesting all that he had remembered. Could these be the images of his sister? Was that why only he saw her and they didn't? The photograph hanging in his hall of himself at the age of four, standing between his father and his mother, who was holding a baby, came to mind. He allowed her features to sink into his subconscious mind. Maybe he had it wrong. Maybe his aunt didn't have a baby after all, as he had been told, but instead, adopted his little sister. The picture must have been taken before she was taken away. His heart raced. Yes, I'll bet that's it. Could this woman be her? He remembered the baby had red hair. And what about the medal? Did it have his mother's initials on it? He wished he had brought it with him.

A look of understanding grew slowly in his eyes. He began to feel more alive and was now sure it must be her reaching out to him. Was she on that ship? Did she give birth aboard the ship? Was this child his niece? *Son of a gun, I'll bet that's it,* he thought. *That's why she found me. She knew this was going to happen. I don't know how, but she had to have known.*

He felt like he was walking into a lion's cage but was not afraid.

It began to rain.

Three Dreams

9:49 p.m. June 5

Prepared for the storm, D.C. walked by in his red watertight suit and boots.

"Better get yours on if you're gonna be out in it. Should be here any time now. She's moving slowly so we'll be in for it for a while."

Chris ran inside the cabin and searched for the manifest. When he found it he read every name carefully. *Her first name is Patty.* His finger ran up and down the list. He regretted having crossed off names as her name might have been deleted by mistake.

Patty. Patty. Shit, there's no Patty on this list. Wait another name for Patty is Patricia. Hmmm! Patricia. His finger ran up and down the list. After several moments of unswerving concentration he found what he was looking for. *Ah, here it is Samuel and Patricia Basque, cabin 1018.* He was ecstatic.

He decided to call the *Sea Star*.

"*Blue Pelican* calling the *Sea Star*. Are you there? Come in. Over.

A voice interrupted the ensuing crackling noise, "*Sea Star* here, over."

"*Sea Star*, this is Chris Healy, Oceanographer with the *National Oceanic and Atmospheric Administration*. What's your location? Over."

The *Sea Star* was a holdover from Vietnam where it was once an evacuation ship that was now transformed into a floating archeological lab.

"Ahoy, Chris. Dr. Weston here…Oceanographer, Adventurer, Master Diver, and Explorer…in any order you want to put 'em," he chuckled. "We're just approaching the sight…and a sad sight, indeed. Hey, you're not the Chris Healy we've all been hearing about, are you? I just can't get my mind around this, first your prediction of the disaster, then a child still alive down there…?" A short pause. "Over."

Ignoring his question he asked, "Have you got any information for us? Over."

"Well, we're not exactly sure yet. Some rain clouds hovering overhead. Should break at any time. Looks like we'll have to get the submersible down quick. Can't risk putting a man down—too rough. It's going to get nastier out here. Once the waves start kicking up we're not going to be able to see much of the bottom. May not be able to put the submersible down if the storm blows in too soon."

Chris knew the submersible was used to penetrate the earth's ocean floor to explore, research, measure and photograph the depths for geographical and geophysical surveys. It had the capacity to go down to 20,000' below the surface and hover like a helicopter. If they could put a diver aboard he could evaluate the *Emperor* through bubble-like portals, a fish bowl in reverse you might say, and relay the information via satellite phone to the top. Its agile mechanical arms can pick almost any object on the sea floor. The nine-foot video arm, with its exterior lights, could easily light up a football field. He hoped it would have already explored the wreck before the storm, and his arrival.

"If it goes down, computer experts will produce a 3-dimensional graphic of the ship so that we can get a better idea of what we're up against. With the oncoming storm the likelihood of putting a diver down now is unlikely. We'll probably use the video arm. We'll have more for you when you get here. What's your ETA? Over."

Chris looked to D.C. for an answer. He held up four fingers of one hand while he stifled a yawn with the other. "About four hours, maybe more. Depends upon what we run up against with upcoming storm. Probably more, from the looks of the weather. Over. Out."

"Roger that. I'll tell ya mate. This is the first time a research program had been assembled to rescue a survivor. It's unprecedented. They don't believe for a minute there's anyone down there alive. We'll be ready for you though," he chuckled. He shook his head like a man that was far from satisfied. "When the scientists aboard first heard they were going to participate, their reaction to the rescue ran from incredulity to outrage.

There isn't a believer in the group. I'd like to see their faces if there is. Over. Out."

The *Sea Star* had already lowered a camera; similar to *Little Alvin*, to scan the ship before the storm fully arrived. Also lowered was a diver who attempted to establish the perimeter of the sunken vessel, but too soon was brought up due to the storm.

Underwater Archeologists, Marine Biologist, scientists, and other experts attempted to coordinate plans for the recovery project while awaiting the *Blue Pelican*. Their surveys, test probes, mapping, and reconnaissance all would assist in outlining the search procedures that would be followed.

The storm was now moving in fast forcing the Search and Rescue helicopter to leave. The *Sea Star* moored next to the buoy set down by the Coast Guard and awaited the storm.

Roberta M. Alleman

2:20 a.m. June 6

It began to rain and the seas were building. Torrents of rain slapped at the *Blue Pelican's* windows with no rhythm at all.

"The wind, W/SW 25/35 knots, with stronger gusts, increasing to 40/50 knots, easing by early morning to 20 to9 25 knots," was broadcast from Honolulu.

Motors churned into action and despite the helmsman best efforts, there was not always a soft landing on the other side of a large wave. The craft, now facing the storm, surmounted each salty hill, which were peaking at 40 feet, and descended its reverse side, with engines running at full power. It pitched, veered, and yawed. Visibility was severely reduced. Broken white water was stretched to the horizon. Occasionally, a substantial spray of water, like a white net of a casting fisherman, surged over her.

Cresting waves struck and shook the *Blue Pelican*. The thrust from the waves lifted their craft over 30 and 40-foot waves, where they paused in midair for a second, and then crashed the boat down on the other side.

Scott was seasick. He went outside and jack knifed himself over the rail to rid himself of his lunch. When the ship suddenly pitched, he lost his balance and found himself being flung into the sea. As he was being hurling through the air, a thought flooded through his mind that this would be the end, the end of life on this earth. He was reconciled to the idea when he hit the water. Incredibly he found himself six feet under with the current carrying him further away from the ship. Flailing his arms, he fought to rise to the surface. As he rose, another wave dumped him and pushed him 15 feet underwater. *My God, they'll never know I'm gone till it's over. I'll be dead by then.* Terror stricken, he vaulted from beneath the wave. He screamed at the top of his lungs, "Help! Help! Man overboard."

The crew was occupied with their own imminent danger and hadn't noticed he had gone overboard.

The shock of the water cleared his brain. *Now don't lose your head*, he told himself. *Wait until you and the boat are on a crest, then scream for all you're worth.* His eyes fastened on the waves that swept toward him.

It took many waves until he finally found himself and the ship cresting on opposite waves together. He screamed, "Man overboard...man overboard," as loud as he could. No one heard him. In-between troughs he was shut out from the view of the boat. Again he waited for the *Blue Pelican* to crest again with him. He began to panic. *What if they never...hear me...find me? What will happen to Marlene?* Suddenly he was thrust high atop a giant wave. He seized the opportunity, "Man overboard, man overboard...port side," he screamed. The sky was dark and the howling wind seemed to sing of ghosts and the ancient dance of dead mariners.

D.C. heard the desperate call and alerted the crew. He peered out looking for him. Too many waves concealed Scott from his view. Winds were blowing at 30 to 40 knots and swells were as high now as 50 feet. He gripped the rail as if he could steady the ship in the wind. Cuppy hastily brought large searchlight topside and swept the waves. As they searched, cold sprays, driven by gusty winds, blew back in their faces in the sort of chill that ran straight into their bones.

"Let go the anchor," a voice yelled against the wind.

"Who the hell is it?"

"Dunno, can't see 'im. Can you?"

"Nah. Can't see shit in this weather."

"There, over there."

"Over where, you idiot."

"There...a little more to your left Cuppy...there...there he is," he said, pointed port side.

"Bring her off the wind. Drop the tires...it should slow us down and keep the transom to the approaching waves. Come round, we'll hook 'im."

"Can't hook 'im, he ain't no fish. Ya'd probably end up spearing 'im with 'im bouncing up and down like a cork. Get the heaving line ya imbecile.'

"That's it, stand on course. Steady man, steady."

"Steady, your ass man, we're in a storm, or don't ya know it?"

"Someone toss a net across the rail."

In the swells, Scott disappeared from their view several times before they got a bead on him.

Below everyone was hurled around like a sack of potatoes, even though they were hanging on. They were being tossed back and forth, back and forth. Before they could get a good hold, they'd be wrenched, once again, from their grip.

Lou yelled, "everybody on the floor. It'll be a bit uncomfortable, but it's the safest place." Those who had already hit the floor just stayed there. Everyone else dropped down and held on to the nearest solid object to keep from sliding across the deck. People were vomiting and moaning. They felt their bodies suspend in mid air while the ship under them dropped suddenly into a trough. A second or two later, their bodies would 'catch up' with the ship and they'd slam into the deck. Most were seasick, battered and all cursed the storm.

Nate had a large gash on the back of his head. Dr. Isu's assistant had a severe laceration on his forehead, which he didn't seem aware of. Sky felt pain in her ankle that spread half way up her calf. Chris laid atop of Dr. Malik in his attempt to keep her stationary. Her face was pale and vomit was oozing out of her mouth. Dr. Isu scooted himself under a low table, crossed his arms over his head, and appeared to be praying. Water began to seep in.

The weather forecast certainly didn't correlate with what they were experiencing now.

Scott could not hear the men above the howling of the wind. He was tiring fast. His wet brow was puckered with fear. His arms ached from waving to attract attention and in keeping him afloat. His throat burned from screaming and having the saltwater deluge his mouth. He felt utter despair, utter helplessness.

Near resigning himself to his fate, he felt something hit his shoulder. He recoiled in fear. A few moments later he felt it again. This time he turned quickly to face his unseen enemy and was jubilant to find a heaving line with a heavy 'monkey fist' on the end.

"Ahoy, grab the line…quickly man."

Scott snatched at the line, and though his fingers were numb, he hung on fast. As he was dragged along he felt the strength of the men pulling him through the water. Sliding under the cresting waves, he feared he'd drown before they could get him aboard. *Now I know what a hooked fish feels like,* he thought. Soon he was along side. With the boat rising and falling beneath their feet, the men had difficulty trying to bring him up. Scott's hands were too numb to climb the net awaiting him. The rolling of the ship slammed his body against the keel several times before he was pulled over the rail.

Three Dreams

"Come on men, bare a hand," someone yelled. Several hands grabbed him and laid his spent body on the deck.

Cuppy pulled his limp body onto his lap. A dry cloth was dabbed at his face.

"You okay buddy," he asked, obviously concerned. "You okay? Say something buddy."

Scott felt the warmth of the people next to him as he drifted in and out of awareness. All he could think to say was, "I'm so hungry that I could eat the sneakers off of a centipede."

"Oh shit," Say Cuppy and he stood abruptly.

You could hear Scott's head hit the deck hard when Cuppy abruptly stood and stomped off. Later, over the storm and howling wind Scott could be heard, retching into the blackness. He spent a good part of an hour jackknifed over the railing calling 'Rolf'. This time he had a safety harness attached to him.

Cuppy smiled.

Roberta M. Alleman

MEANWHILE 28 MILES AWAY

Phil's boat was in trouble. In places, the wind was blowing at 50 knots. It squalled so hard that it blew wave tops nearly flat and streams of spume were coming off of them. The air was thick with salt.

Down below the men donned foul-weather gear, life jackets, and safety harnesses in preparation of abandoning ship. They had not sent out a SOS, as it would be impossible to be heard over the howling gales. The waves were tossing the 60-foot yacht as if it were a toy. In anticipation of increasing wind they had already lashed the boom to the deck, just clear of the life rafts. The storm jib had already been torn loose but still provided enough windage to move the yacht. They sent up flares hoping they'd be seen by a craft nearby. Now it was a waiting game.

Throughout, the skipper maintained a perpetual smile on his face. Phil wondered if he hadn't been struck with some disease that caused the Cheshire cat smile and it made him nervous. The old man seemed to take everything in stride. If he was scared, he showed no indication. Only he knew the storm was helping him. The winds were blowing him in the direction of the wreck sight.

Earlier Phil had informed the passenger of the skipper's past experience as an accomplished skipper. This enabled the men to feel a little more comfortable in knowing that they were in good hands. He seemed to anticipate what was going to happen before it did. With that, Phil thought if anyone would get them through this, it would be his friend.

Then came a sickening wood splintering crash at the hull, seemingly at the water line. The men hurried topside to see what they had hit. Nothing was within sight. A quick inspection of the keel revealed minimal damage. Quickly they sealed up the damaged area. Upon returning, they found water was now sloshing into the cabin, the batteries had short-circuited and the radio was no longer working. They had already given up on sending more flares as the ones that were sent up earlier were carried away at an alarming speed due to the high winds. They were out there alone now. It was then that the skipper decided to steer the boat in the direction of the edge of the storm.

The situation was grave.

Roberta M. Alleman

6:07 a.m. June 6

The storm raged for hours. Although battered, the *Sea Star* rode it out, double moored as they were. The rain stopped suddenly as light was beginning to flood the sky, but the wind howled on for another hour.

The buoy marking the *Emperor's* resting place held true during the storm and now lazily bobbed under the oil droplets and silvery air bubbles rising to the surface. Knowing this was the spot where the liner went down, a few of the crew made the sign of the cross while others said a silent prayer while others stood silent and white with shock.

The *Blue Pelican* slid past a compacted mass of fresh wreckage of mattresses, life jackets, floor tiles, chairs, paneling, dead fish, clothing, and other debris that were washing to and fro in the current. They were traveling, seemingly, neither one way nor the other. They were, to all intents, stationary. Voices toned away to mere whispers as they passed through. Everyone looked at each other uneasily as they stood silently at the rails. They could only wonder what those last moments must have been like.

Overhead a returning helicopter, looking like a giant dragonfly, searched for survivors in the widespread debris caused by the storm.

The men from Search and Rescue were already fishing bodies and debris from the waves using long poles with hooks at the end. Their strained, cold, sad faces coupled with the setting of their jaw made it plain they would not give up easily. They were professionals showing compassion and solicitude for the deceased. It was doubted if anyone had survived the wreck, let alone survive the storm as well but still they went about their tasks quietly looking for some signs of life.

The silence was eerie.

Soon the team on the *Blue Pelican's* began seeing thicker oil slicks as they headed to into the current. A short time later they located and rendezvoused with the *Sea Star*. Their vivid coloring stood out stark against the slate sea and angry horizon where they were moored alongside the red buoy.

Suddenly the body of a man dressed in a tuxedo popped up. All who saw him stopped what they were doing. Some made the sign of

Three Dreams

the cross. For a few moments they just stared at him. The silence was broken when one of the captains yelled, "Get that man out of the water." A diver jumped in, placed his arm around his waist and whispered to him, "It's okay, we've got you now. We'll take care of you." Gently he towed him over to one of the rescue boats, careful to keep his head above water. The diver gave a caveman grunt as he pushed him along side of the craft. Several men reached in and painstakingly pulled him aboard where they laid him next to other recovered victims. He was examined by a doctor and pronounced dead. They searched for identification before the Coast Guard Chaplain said a prayer and he was placed in a body bag. Today they had recovered three hundred thirteen victims so far. They knew, with the storm, bodies were probably now drifting over a hundred square miles.

Chris' eyes met those of the Captain across the waves. The Captain gave him thumbs up. His expression, and the look in his eyes said, *we're pulling for you.* He understood too well the magnitude of the problems these men were facing. Understanding, Chris nodded his head.

There was a scurry of preparation as the men, still in their red and yellow slickers, rechecked the equipment for damage after the storm. The ship was now astir with organized frenzy. After viewing what they just saw, the whole affair had a new urgent complexion.

When they neared the scene they noticed four boats had arrived before them. Obviously their boats were faster than the *Blue Pelican's* was or they had a better time of it through the storm, although no one could figure out how. Several miles away yachts, motor launches, sail boats and other crafts of various sizes were also speeding toward the wreckage sight. Within the hour many had arrived. Among them was Phil's boat.

Ever so many wanted to help, to hear if the child had been rescued, while a handful just wanted to see where the liner went down. A few morbid others leaned over the side and snagged a piece of floating debris for a souvenir. The Coast Guard could be heard warning them, through a loud speaker, not to remove any keepsakes from the area and to stay back from the site. While some boats heeded the warning, others did not. As they came closer the Coast Guard threatened to fire a shot across their bow if they didn't desist. Those who had removed items quickly tossed their 'trophies' back in and returned to the boundary set by the rescuers.

Phil's boat, making it through the storm, pulled along side of the *Blue Pelican*. He jumped aboard, anxious to find out if there was any late breaking news. He was sad to hear there was none. Thinking those below would know more he headed for the cabin. Just as he entered Dr. Weston, aboard the *Sea Star,* was radioing the *Blue Pelican*. He asked for Chris specifically. Everyone stopped talking.

"Dr. Healy, this is Dr. Weston…I don't believe it. They don't believe it. Then again, maybe it's not what we think at all. Maybe it's just something scraping against something…" He chuckled between words, as if he had just heard the world's funniest joke.

Impatient, Chris interrupted, "This is Dr Healy. What the hell are you babbling about man?

"You're not going to believe it. We're checking to be sure if what we found is real. I mean…we dropped a microphone down to the ship. The stories about you guys and a baby, well…we thought it was a joke and we were going to pull a joke on *you* by showing you there was nothing down there…well the joke's on us…just listen." Then faintly, "Whaaagh, Whaaagh," came over the speaker. Although faint it did sound like a child crying.

The room broke into a roar of laughter and cheering. They were ecstatic. Everyone slapped each other on the back in congratulations. Many were laughing and crying at the same time.

"Quiet, quite," said Dr Isu. "Let hear what he has to say."

"We checked and rechecked our findings and it seems what you said all along is true…it's overwhelmingly confirmed. Think we didn't have some red faces over here? And they thought it was absurd. Well, the joke's on them." He hardly bothered to lower his voice at all. "There is a child down there. It must be in some air pocket. They can't determine exactly where it is; only that it's astern. It broke in two when it sank and they're sure the voice is coming from there. So what do you think now doctor? There's one redeeming factor…you were right all along. No matter how cockamamie it may have sounded, you followed through, and here we are, ready to rescue a baby…all because you men wouldn't give in to ridicule. You're all heroes ya know. Over."

Again cheers broke out. People were hugging each other and slapping Chris, Lou and Scott on the back.

Three Dreams

"Good job."
"Fantastic man."
"Well done."
"You were right. You're the man."
"Thank you for the information. We're certainly glad to hear it…and thank your team. They deserve the credit. We're getting a lunch ready and should be boarding you in about ten to twenty minutes to get the particulars. Over. Out."

Lou, Scott and Chris could not help themselves. They were grinning from ear to ear. They shook hands strongly, but cordially after hugging one other. A sense of relief fell over them. Until then, they were never sure about the dreams. Now they felt as though they had just shed 100 pounds of weight off of their shoulders.

Acting on the information he just heard and the break down from Lou about the chamber, Phil bolted for the door. In a matter of moments he was back aboard his boat preparing to broadcast worldwide, in millions of homes, in every country with a satellite dish, cable, antenna, a radio, or TV.

He waved to crowd.

They waved and smiled, hoping for good news.

Phil had recorded the conversation and the cries of the child. "Do you hear that ladies and gentlemen? Those are the cries of a tiny infant who is trapped below in the bowels of the sunken ship, *Emperor*, who, just a few hours ago was brought to the bottom by a Tsunami, taking 1828 passengers and crew with her. This child, crying out to be saved, is the only known survivor of this terrible disaster, which can only be compared to that of the *Titanic*. I am recording live ladies and gentlemen, on the very spot where the *Emperor* went down. At this very moment preparations, led by Doctor Chris Healy, are being made to bring this child to the surface. I cannot tell you ladies and gentlemen of the electricity being felt here at the rescue site. You may ask how are they going to bring the child to the surface? Well, Mr. Lou Davis, an inventor has created a special carrier, and who also, incidentally, predicted this disaster and rescue. This carrier is self-sustaining and is air and watertight. It will supply the warmth the child needs to survive through the cold waters below, and it will supply the correct amount of oxygen it will also need for the journey to the surface. You can imagine the anticipation fellow hopefuls here are experiencing while praying for the safe rescue of the child. Many have come many miles and through storms to be a part of this wondrous event. Miracles do happen, ladies and gentlemen. Stay tuned to station TXXM and it's affiliates for the latest breaking news."

When the broadcast was finished, Phil returned to the *Blue Pelican*. He wanted to be nearby for any late breaking news, or so he told himself. Actually he was worried sick about the child and thought everyone was too casual about the rescue. He wanted everything to happen *now*, but as a journalist, he learned to bide his time, no matter what he really thought.

The *Blue Pelican* dispatched their motorized rubber raft with key rescuers aboard twenty minutes later.

As they approached the 174-foot research ship, their eyes traveled to the submersible that carried cameras and lighting equipment, which was being prepared to be loaded aboard of the *Sea Star*. The rear of the ship was like a miniature harbor with electric doors that would be sealed shut after she had been secured until her next venture.

When they boarded, Dr. Weston met them. He was a heavy-set man with keen blue eyes that looked out of a deeply tanned face. "Welcome aboard. I am Dr. Weston, your unofficial host for today. And who might Dr. Healy be," he asked with a slight German accent, as he scanned their faces. He was dressed in cut-off Levi's, a T-shirt, and beat up sneakers. His salt and pepper hair looked like it just went through a wind tunnel and his mustache was in dire need of a trim. His eyelids drooped as if he had just awakened or was on the verge of sleep. His chin supported a goatee.

"That would be me," said Chris. The two men shook hands in a friendly way.

"A pleasure doctor…a pleasure." While shaking hands, Dr Weston looked at Chris keenly for a few moments, as if he was checking to see if he had three eyes in the middle of his forehead, or if his head would spin 180 degrees on his neck. Finally letting go, he said, "Ah, let me take you on the grand tour of the old lady."

On deck, placed in their perspective compartments were: a side scan sonar, a deep tow camera, immersion suits, a remotely controlled camera sled, wet suits, flippers, diving gear of every sort, cameras of various sizes, and other equipment that would aid in their research. A recompression camber lay like a beached whale upon her deck; next to air tanks were hoses, and more diving gear.

Finally he escorted them into the field laboratory. The room was warm, comfortable, and sterile. An impressive assortment of control and recording systems, sonar, radio direction finder, listening devices and other electronic equipment covered two walls of the room. On the third wall were charts of oceans of the world. On the fourth wall was a myriad of video screens, a few of which were viewing the *Emperor* at that very moment.

"As you see, we have located the *Emperor*. When we send out the submersible we tape everything it sees. What you're looking at now is a tape."

As he spoke several people began filing into the room. One member whispered to the group and they all began laughing: this was clearly a group joke.

Turning, Dr Weston waved his arm toward the men. As he did, an issue of *Notices to Mariners* was seen jutting from his pants pocket. "Gentlemen, these are the key people you will need to speak with. They will help evaluate the feasibility of your rescue attempt. Together I know you will have more understanding of what you're up against." He introduced everyone, and then left the room.

They all shook hands, as they looked each other over. Tension was broken when someone yelled, "Let's eat."

Everyone took seats around a large conference table that was piled with frankfurters, buns, various sodas, cold cuts, a greenish looking potato salad, Cole Slaw and various plastic knives and forks.

After lunch tapes were watched, charts were analyzed, scenarios were discussed and verbal walk-through of the rescue were gone over. Lou explained the workings of the chamber, to the astonishment of the scientists, who had many questions about its capabilities for their research.

In the end, all were in agreement that the child would probably be found in the infirmary, but alternative areas were also discussed.

"How do you know it's really a child? Couldn't the sound be coming off of something else," the whisperer asked.

"Good question. As you know," one man said, looking embarrassed, "we didn't think there was a child, however, our instruments can detect the different audio frequencies from any species in the world. We tested and retested and came to the same conclusion, the sound is definitely a human species, probably a child."

"How did you come to that conclusion," asked Lou.

"We dropped a microphone down to the ship. Of course we thought all of this was a big joke...you guys...the baby...." Uncomfortable, the man cleared his voice. "Well, we were going to rib you about it so we dropped the microphone just to show you it wasn't human, but perhaps metal. We...ah...noises of settling, loose metal scraping with the current or...." His voice dropped off.

"Well—besides our instruments, our ship's doctor put an end to that thinking. He swore that was the voice of a newborn. Guess he should know. He's delivered over 2,300 babies in his life time," added one of the scientists.

Everyone laughed.

In between their articulate presentation, *the whisperer,* a husky diver who looked inscrutable, sat in on their discussions. He continuously probed Chris with questions that were unrelated to the rescue. Chris kept his cool until the young man insinuated he was looking for a name for himself. It was obvious both teams were tolerating his presence because he was the ship's master diver and would lead the team to rescue Chris, should there be a need. The young man ended by saying, "are you sure it's a baby?"

Chris didn't respond, but instead, wondered how long it would take him to sever through this big mouth's jugular vein with a plastic knife.

"Are you sure it's not," Chris said instead, his eyes glued on the diver.

Startling everyone, one man stood so suddenly that his chair fell over. "Let me interrupt for a moment. Cal, you either shut the hell up and pay attention, or you can get the hell out of here. Your business is rescue, and to pay attention. Lives depend it. You **can** be replaced you know," the scientist said with emphasis. He then turned to the group and apologized. His eyes never moved off of Cal as picked up his chair and sat down.

"Look...you think we're going to put our reputations on the line and tell you something we're not sure of?" Nods of agreement came from his colleagues. "Our microphones can pick up whale calls hundreds of miles away. We carry sophisticated instruments, which enable us, simply put, to decipher one sound from another. That is definitely a human voice down there. Our vocal chords are like no other animal because of those vocal chords. I don't know how this child remained and still remains alive. We think it's in an air pocket.

Three Dreams

That's the only answer for a ship that's been broken in two. God was watching out for the tyke that day." Again his fellow comrades nodded in agreement. "Now let's get busy, time is running out. With her…or him…crying, he or she is eating up oxygen more rapidly."

"When was the last time you heard her," asked Cuppy.

"Her…it's a her?"

"We really don't know for sure at this point. So when was it?"

"About five minutes before you came aboard. We don't know if we'll hear it again, so again, let's get busy."

They wound up by showing them the diving gear they would be wearing during the rescue and what to do if this or that happened.

Chris's team had already worked out most of the particulars that they had run down to the scientists. Throughout, they listened, nodding occasionally, testing an argument with a question now and then. Graphs, charts, and images were pored over. When they terminated the meeting everyone felt they had a good grasp of what lay ahead.

Pointing to the minuscule one and a half-inch antenna that was mounted on the helmet, the radioman said, "There's obviously no track record for this device. I just put it together." He grinned, ear to ear. This little dickens here will bounce off a pair of satellites in geostationary orbit above the equator." He raised his chin and gave it a toss in the direction of the satellites. "The signal stays with you men, no matter where you go, aboard the ship. You'll have to play it by ear, no pun intended. We'll help you as much as we can from up here. I understand you'll be in touch with your ship, and not ours. Is that right?"

"Well, yes," says Chris. "We never thought…."

"Don't worry, I'll ride back with you and act as radio man. I know this apparatus better than anyone. If anything goes wrong, you'll need me there."

Roberta M. Alleman

Back Aboard the *Blue Pelican*

Later, while Chris was standing at the rail of the *Blue Pelican* staring into an infinity of sky and vast ocean, Phil contemplated approaching him. He was enveloped in a yellow wet suit and seemed to be in deep thought as he stared at the boats that were moored around the perimeter. There must have been well over 100 of them. The air was pleasantly warm. The breeze, after the rain, was refreshing.

After a few moments, Phil decided now was the time to speak with him.

"Excuse me Chris. Is it all right to intrude?"

"Sure Phil, what is it?"

"Well…ah…many years ago…I had a little girl who died of crib death." He coughed softly. "I've never quite recovered from it ya know. This child…this helpless child only reminds me of her…you know…with the birthmark and all. You see, she had one in the same place," he laughed nervously. "Of course I don't think it's her, come back…it's just…." He reached into the inside pocket of his jacket and withdrew his wallet. Inside was a cellophane pocket containing the withered white rose he had removed from her casket. With trembling hands, he handed it to Chris.

"Would you carry this with you when you go? Maybe…er…maybe it'll bring you and the little tyke good luck or somethin'."

Chris could see the pleading in his eyes and accepted the rose.

"Of course Phil. I'm sorry to hear about your daughter. I know you must miss her."

"Yes, yes I do. Her name was Rose, named after my wife's favorite flower," he said, forcing a smile.

Carefully Chris placed it inside his wetsuit. He felt strongly that Phil believed, deep down, that this was his child reincarnated, but did not try to discourage him.

"Oh, by the way. Sky asked me to give you this. Thought you might need it…for good luck too."

Placed in Chris's hand was the medal the dancer had given him. Eagerly he tried to turn it over; seeking the initials he hoped would be there, but instead turned it 360-degrees in his excitement. He cursed under his breath and tried again. The initials engraved in it were *MH*. He wanted to kiss Phil. "Phil, You don't know what this means to me. Thank you, thank you ever so much my man."

"I think I do. As much to you as that rose does to me." Phil clasped his hand, stood and looked at him for a moment, then turned to leave.

"Don't worry Phil, she'll be okay," says Chris, softly.

Phil nodded and walked toward the motorized rubber raft waiting to take him to his boat. Another broadcast was scheduled to air in fifteen minutes.

Chris placed the medal next to the rose within the safety of his wet suit. He patted the area outside to insure it stayed in place.

Soon it was time to go. As the men prepared to dive, all became quiet.

Gathered together, someone said, "Shouldn't we say a prayer or something?"

Dr. Malik stepped up and placed her hands on Chris and Cuppy's shoulders.

"Lord. Guide these men in rescuing one of your children from the depths," prayed Dr. Malik. "Guide them in doing Thy work. Bring them all back to us, safe and sound. Thy will, not ours, be done. We thank you Lord and ask for your blessing on this day. Amen."

A murmur of 'Amen' rippled through the group.

Holding their masks secure the search team back-rolled off the rear of the ship.

8:29 a.m. June 6

Twice Sky waved as the divers bobbed in the water clearing their masks. She summoned a small smile so Chris wouldn't know how fearful she felt. She thought she shouldn't let him go, and yet, realistically, what choice did she have. *Don't go,* a small voice whispered from within. She framed him in a gaze that excluded everyone else. They stared at each other intently for a moment, and then he gave her a slight smile before he was gone.

On their wrists the divers wore a fabric banded automatic timer, which would start timing the length of the dive at 3 to 5 feet. The band, attached to the timer, passed under both watchband pins of the instrument and was vital in informing the men of how much time they had left.

The seven divers started down the descending line one by one. At 80 feet Chris checked his depth gauge, but the *Emperor* was still not in sight. The reality of the disaster had not come up to meet them yet.

With pressure increasing every second and the greenish dark closing around them they reached the 100-foot mark. The only sounds were those of their breathing. Pressure built up in their ears. They swallowed and it cleared in a series of pops and squeals, then they dove another 50 feet.

As they hovered weightless over the dimly lit ocean desert, they finally spotted the E*mperor*. They saw the ship had broken in two. The fore half was laying with a starboard list. The stern, a mangled heap of metal and buckled structures, came to rest about 100 meters away. Steel decks had fallen into each other. Tangled girders and steel plates were almost unrecognizable. Passageways were full of torn steel. Decks above were supported by nothing in particular. Fifty meters away laid her propeller, fully intact. Her blocks, although twisted, still held a few of her lifeboats. Nearby the anchor chain had fallen in a heap giving it the illusion of a sleeping sea snake. An explosion had ripped open her sides flattening many of her decks giving her the appearance that she had been stomped on by a giant foot. Saltwater had flooded into her, breaking engines, machinery, and heavy equipment from their bolts, leaving them to smash through the ship's bulkheads and compartments on their way to the ocean floor.

Three Dreams

Other areas were misshapen or crushed beyond recognition. Giant steel plates had buckled and ruptured on both sides. A lone lifeboat, held erect by one of the ship's ladders, was almost twisted beyond recognition. It was a poignant reminder that there were no survivors.

Scattered about the gloom of the sea bed were unattached remnants of other peoples lives: a woman slipper, an intricately engraved leather purse, a splintered bed half buried in the sand, a silver framed picture of an elderly couple and a wedding veil, which flowed softly in the current. Furniture, luggage, crockery, and dishes with elegant patterns lay scattered along the bottom, many still intact. Men, women and children were strewn indiscriminately across the abyss below. Many were beginning to fill with gas. Everyone knew, when that happened, they would rise to the top, but for only a short time. They would then sink below again, and be forever lost.

They had seen the characteristic long, round, white tipped pectoral fins of the oceanic sharks at about 130 feet. Their reputation of congregating around mid-ocean disasters only reinforced the finality of what they were witnessing. Absorbing the grim sight, they exchanged glances, and then moved ahead.

Someone said, "Watch out for those guys. They don't care if you're living or dead when they're hungry."

Scrutinizing the bottom with a cursory eye, Nate said, almost to himself, "I wonder if this is what the *Titanic* looked like when she sunk."

Their eyes searched for details as they swam closer. Several bodies lay trapped under debris, arms floating loosely with the current as if directing an unseen orchestra. As they moved past the tangled masses of metal and collapsed walkways, jagged pieces of the wreck protruded ominously. From beneath the sand a stingray suddenly darted from the protection of his camouflage, startling the men. Surprised, Cuppy dropped his light, but dove quickly to retrieve it.

At the moment he reached for it, there was a loud booming sound, which made the ship shudder. A large boiler rolled off the ship where it had been precariously balanced since the wreck. They knew instinctively the boom was due to the buckling of the ship's huge steel plates either by loss of air, or the ship's settling.

"Watch out," the divers yelled out, pointing above him.

Cuppy looked up. Loose debris and sand poured over him. Thinking quickly, he remembered, to exert power under water, one has to empty their lungs. Exhaling his breath, he lunged to one side, just seconds before it could crush him. Hitting the floor of the seabed with a muffled thud, the boiler then rolled across the bottom and came to rest against the once melodic piano.

"It's creepy if you ask me…like crawling into another's grave," he says, "Maybe that's not where we're supposed to start out the search." He stared into the black hole of a companionway and couldn't help but morbidly comparing it with a tomb…perhaps his own. He rolled over to blow a trace of water out of his facemask.

Ignoring him Chris says, "We'll each take a section. You four start looking around over there," pointing to the stern, "and you three come with me. That's the section where sick bay is located, so let's start over there." Earlier he had noticed a passageway that was on the same level as the infirmary that appeared to be reasonably free of wreckage. The second team gave them a thumb up and moved toward deeper water.

Cuppy checked his knife and the crabbing hook that would help him pull himself along, over and through the wreck. Now ready, he took a deep breath for luck and followed his friend. The two remaining divers followed close behind.

When they reached the ship's structure, Chris shifted the carrier to his left hand. Thinking it cumbersome, he decided to attach it to his weight belt with a cord, knowing he was going to need both hands to get through the rubble.

His narrowed eyes darted in all directions, trying to peer through the darkness of the corridors. Turning their lamps back and forth, they found there was more wreckage than they thought.

Finding a good place to enter, they filed one-by-one into the blackness, their lamps leaving a trail of luminescent bubbles behind them.

The deeper they went into the bowels of the ship the more rubble they encountered. Moving carefully, they climbed over broken paneling, torn wires and cables, bent pipes, torn steel and other debris. Pushing and pulling they made their way deeper and deeper. Occasionally one of them would curse when they were gashed by some projection, or had fallen over debris. Otherwise the only thing they heard was each other's breathing. As they went they passed a series of closed cabin doors. They inspected within then marked the door with a large 'X' indicating it was cleared. In the event they needed rescuing themselves, these X's would lead the rescuers to them. A *trail of bread crumbs*, Cuppy called it.

Nothing was familiar to Chris. In his dream there was neither rubble nor the appearance of an occasional body. Their hands reached out for them with gnarled fingers. Their eyes stared blankly out of the onset of bloating skin, which was beginning to look like wrinkled tissue paper. They were shaken when they found a woman in a wedding dress and a man in a tuxedo, clutched in a death embrace. Her hair floated gently, her mouth frozen in a silent scream. Their thoughts went to the veil that they had seen swaying in the current. Had they married before the disaster, they wondered.

"Poor devils," someone said softly.

Suddenly pieces of paneling and other debris pulled loose from the ceiling, knocking Chris off his feet. A heavy object fell across his wrist, knocking the lamp out of his hand. It fell away, flickered and then went out.

The darkness had swallowed him. It was pitch black. Protecting the carrier against himself, he pressed his body to the floor. It felt like all the floors from above were crashing around him. Then all was quiet.

Chris lay there for a few moments, waiting to see if more debris would fall.

"You guys okay," Chris called through his microphone. No response. "Hey, you guys okay?" Nothing. Hoping they may be on the other side of the heap, and okay, he yelled, "Ahoy…you guys…ahoy." No response. Thinking they may be trapped under the debris, after the first frenzy of indiscriminate searching, he began systematically probing for his friends. Frantic, he fumbled about, but the only thing he felt was the current moving to and fro. Willing all of his senses into his brain for processing, he reasoned they were either under all of that debris, or they were alive, but on the other side of the choked opening. At any rate, communication was severed and it was pitch black.

Suddenly he felt there was a presence nearby but was afraid to reach out, for fear of finding a dead comrade, but quickly reasoned it couldn't be. He reasoned a wall of debris separated them. Of that he hoped was true.

Eerily, he sensed it was moving toward him and reached for the knife.

Roberta M. Alleman

Owl-eyed, his head snapped around with predatory speed.

Something or someone was out there in the dark…he knew it. His fear made him feel like a helpless child. Feeling the presence, his mind began to imagine some large creature slithering along the passageway, toward him.

When his hand found the knife his fingers tightened around its hilt. Something thumped into him. He screamed. Bubbles escaped his mask. The impulse to escape surged through him. Arching his back, he turned and stabbed out viciously, legs kicking wildly, and slashed at the unseen assailant. Drawing in great gulps of air he tried to back away from the large jaws of some yet undiscovered sea monster. Terrorized, his pulse thumped loudly in his ears. His eyes tried to pierce through the ray less pitch-black jungle to see where the next attack might come from. Working on pure instinct and adrenaline, he struck out again and again until finally, he sank his knife deeply into the flesh of his opponent. The form fell away.

Squatting on his heels, he frantically groped for the light, stirring up sediment as he searched headlong about his feet. Finally his hand closed around the grip. Swiftly he switched it on. Nothing. Gasps were escaping his dry mouth. He jabbed the switch off and on, off and on. Nothing. He banged it against his palm and shook it again. It flickered. He banged it harder. The area lit up. He quickly pushed to his feet and shined the light in the monster's direction. To his horror there was no monster at all, but a corpse moving with the drift of the water, midway between the floor and overhead. He looked like he was participating in some magician's trick. His emaciated face was discolored and showed signs that hungry fish had already discovered him. The eyes were glazed and unblinking. Scott's knife still protruded from his chest.

Both relieved and horrified by what he had done, tremors swept over him. He wondered where the corpse had come from but finally resolved it had probably fallen through the paneling, perhaps from an upper floor. After staring at his 'opponent' for a few moments he gingerly removed his knife then pushed the corpse gently away with the back of his arm.

He would find later, as he fought, he had lost the timer from his wrist when one of the pins broke off and that the alarm, which would notify him when he was low on air, was jammed.

Three Dreams

With his sole source of help unavailable he continued to probe forward through the gauntlet of darkness. He inched his way down the passageway. Searched compartment doors were marked with an X, or if already open, one was placed on the bulkhead next to it. The interiors were a ghostly place.

Cuts stung his hands and legs as he removed items along his way. Moving cautiously, eyes darting about and hands outstretched, he moved as careful as he would if he were in a lion's den.

Soon he entered a section where the floor was now the ceiling. It was eerie. *Hmmm. They didn't tell me about this,* he thought. He could have easily become confused with which direction was up, were it not for his bubbles rising up to the passageway 'floor.' He'd stop periodically and look at his map, hoping he was following the right passages to the infirmary. His lamp cut through the surprisingly clear water within this part of the ship. He could hear his heart pounding as he shook off the cold that was permeating his wet suit. He passed one hatchway, then another. He knew instinctively that his air was running out. He checked his timer, only to find that now it was missing. Minutes were ticking by.

Unable to find Chris, the men, unhurt, returned to the ship. They hope he was alive and would contact the ship as to his well-being.

On deck Cuppy gave Sky a nod then hurried to the door. Before exiting he heard Dr. Isu ask, "What is it Scott?"

Silence gathered in the room.

He glanced over at Scott. A shadow had crossed his face. His mouth was open, soundless: suddenly he looked like he was in a trance, and began to nod his head. He seemed far away.

"What is it," Cuppy asked again.

"I can see Chris. He's hurt. He needs help."

He drew the eyes of everyone in the room.

"Where is he, in the ship…where? What do mean hurt? How bad is it?" His nerves tightened.

"Yes, in the ship. He has a concussion…a bad one, I'm afraid."

"Does he have the child," asked Dr. Malik.

"No, he can't locate her."

"Can you help him?" Cuppy gave him a faint smile of confidence and encouragement as he fought for self-control.

"I don't know…I don't know."

"Try Scott. Try to reach him with your mind."

Scott tried to concentrate: to talk to Chris within his mind. He was astounded at the remarkable vividness of the vision that was beginning to appear. Previously they had only been flashing pictures. Now it was like he was standing beside Chris. Was it a waking dream or just a hallucination…or was it real? It frightened him a little.

He was on his feet in the next instant, "Get up. You've got to get up Chris."

Startled, Chris looked around for Scott, thinking he had been found. "Where are you? I was never so glad to hear anyone in my life." He flashed his light around, but couldn't locate him.

"Where the hell are you?"

"I'm aboard ship."

"What? Aboard shi…" Chris thought he was losing it. "Beginning to hallucinate. I'm worse than I thought."

Curiosity was replaced by watchful concern by the team. Lucky ran outside and returned moments later with everyone else. Sky watched with a kind of fascination as she regarded Lou's face.

"Get up Chris. Do it! Do it now!"

"I don't know where you really are…I can't move. I can't muster the strength to move from here." Pain was the only thing he grasped. His skull ached. He briefly shut his eyes, waiting for the pounding to go away.

"Yes you can Chris. You must try. You've got to try. You're low on air."

"I can't locate the child in this maze."

"I'll help you Chris, but first, you have to get on your feet."

Reluctantly he tried. He stumbled and fell a few times but was finally able to keep himself erect. He leaned against a wall for support. He stood there for a few moments, and then moved on.

"Good. Now move down the corridor to your left. Do you see where the breakfast cart has turned over? She's just on the other side of it. Point your torch up. See where it says infirmary?"

Chris pointed his lamp to the left. "I see it," he said weakly.

"Go. Go now." Scott could see Chris was running out of air and time. He knew he'd never make it to the surface alive but did not inform the others. He had to give his friend hope.

"Go Chris…down the corridor to the cart. She's there. You're so close. Go now."

Three Dreams

    Nervous, Cuppy shifted from foot to foot, yet he couldn't tear himself away. His eyes were full of questions.

Roberta M. Alleman

9:51 a.m. June 6

Chris's vision was blurred. He could barely see the cart. Out of the dimness his eyes searched for details. He stumbled forward. Moments later he could make out its outline. His heart began to beat faster. He quickened his movements and was soon at the infirmary door.

He approached the cart and attempted to move it away but was startled to find how difficult it was to move it only a few feet. Finally he was able to push it aside. He tried the handle and pushed against the door. It wouldn't budge. He pushed again.

"Try hard Chris."

"Yes, try hard," Phil repeated. He couldn't know that Chris couldn't hear him.

"If you can do better, get your skinny ass down here and you do it." His voice was uneven with fatigue.

"What's he doing," blurted Cuppy.

"He's outside the infirmary and is trying to jar the door loose."

"Is the baby okay?"

"Don't know, he hasn't gotten in yet."

"Is he okay," asked Sky, afraid of the answer?

"He'll be okay," Scott lied. Then the vision was gone.

Chris inhaled deeply, and then hurled himself at the door. He heard the catch ungrip. He pushed harder. The water pressure on the other side wouldn't allow entrance. He pushed again; finally the door began to give. After several more thrusts, he was in.

10:03 a.m. June 6

The room was exactly as he had seen it in his dreams. The hands were holding the child above the water, which was rising quickly. He stood transfixed for a moment, and then realized he had to work fast. He balanced the chamber atop a medicine cabinet that was bolted to the wall and reached for the child.

As soon as he took the infant the hands sank beneath the water. He submerged his head to see where they had gone. They were nowhere to be seen.

He summoned into his mind that he must place this child into the container but he couldn't recall what he was supposed to do next. Then he remembered the green button. He pushed it and the lid snapped loose. He opened the small life sustaining receptacle the rest of the way, then placed her carefully inside as if he had been trained by the bomb squad. Remembering the rose Phil had given him; he searched inside his wet suit and found it just where he had put it. "This is for good luck, Rose." Gazing at her for a few moments he noticed silken stands of fine red hair on her head. *Just like your mom had.* He then placed the rose next to her tiny feet and covered her with the pink blanket someone had thoughtfully included. *I like that...Rose*, he thought. *I hereby name you Rose. After all, I am your uncle.*

He couldn't recall what Lou had said about closing it, so he pushed the only button on that side that he could see. The lid closed and small lights illuminated on the bottom of the chamber. He could hear a soft hum emanating from the bottom. His heart gave a delirious thump of exhilaration, but he somehow resisted the impulse to shout. He was too exhausted to cheer, even mentally. *I guess I did it right,* he thought. *I've got eight minutes. Now, how do I get out of here?*

Before leaving the cabin Chris turned to take a last look. The cabin was completely filled with water now. Unnoticed before, he discovered a slender woman that was trapped beneath the examining table. She was wearing a pink negligee, which flowed in harmony with her red hair and the current. His instinct was to release her from the death grip, but he knew that would take time, and time he did not have.

Roberta M. Alleman

He stared at her for a few moments and felt a deep sadness inside with having to leave her behind. *I never got to know you, and now....*

Close by, and also trapped beneath the table, was, who he thought to be a nurse, due to her white shoes and what little he could see of a nurse's uniform. He hesitated, but knew it was too late for the both of them.

Chris looked once more at the sister he never knew. "How did you know? How could you have known beforehand that this is where we'd meet?" He stared at her as if she'd answer. Realizing time was waning he said, "Good-bye Sis. I'll take good care of my niece for you. She won't want for anything you can believe that. You rest now." Tears formed in his eyes. He groped desperately for an answer of how she possibly could have known this was going to be her fate. How did she find him? How did she know he would be the one to save her child? Did she search for him? So many questions that only she could answer. He could never know.

10:14 a.m. June 6

As he fumbled his way down the passageway, nests of questions were buzzing through his brain. Suddenly his light went out. In his attempt to turn it on, he lost his grip of the chamber but in one rattlesnake-quick motion he scooped it back into his arms before it dropped to the floor. He stood there, heart pounding, while he held the warm chamber to his chest. "Cripes, not now," he yelled as he shook the lamp with his free hand. He miserably flipped the switch on, off, on, off. Still, it didn't work. "God-damn piece of shit," he scorned the light, his eyes pinpoints of barely controlled rage. Time was slipping away. Sickness rose over him in an overwhelming wave, which was followed by white lights. Disgusted, he threw the lamp down. The pitch black was absolute...and frightening. Fear clutched at the pit of his stomach. *Which way do I go?*

Suddenly to his left he could see a light, not as the light of a lamp, but a wavering luminescent light, like, but oh! How different the light looked, than that of a candle. He watched it for a few moments, but nothing happened. Motionless and fascinated he thought it had some purpose in its visitation. It was as though it was waiting for him. He began to move toward it. As he moved closer, it moved away. *I think it's leading me,* he thought.

He groped along the passageway holding the child close to his chest to protect the infant and for the warmth. As he hurried, he fell headlong over something in his path. He protected the tiny box by holding it aloft as he thumped to the floor. Something struck him hard on the head. "God damn it, not again," he cried. He lay there panting, feeling nauseated and dizzy. Unable to gather enough strength to rise to his feet, minutes began to stack up like glaciers in winter. His head throbbed. He wondered if he hadn't received a concussion. His hands and feet were now swollen and insensitive, from the cold. The Helium he was breathing was a substitute for nitrogen that diluted his oxygen for deep water diving. Now it was the very thing that was draining him of his body heat.

Roberta M. Alleman

10:29 a.m. June 6

Suddenly his earphones came to life. "Sir, can you hear me?" Chris almost jumped out of his skin. He did not recognize the voice.

Topside, all eyes were glued to the radio as with one mind as they had been for more than an hour and a half.

"Yes, I can hear you." His voice came quiet, childlike in its tone. He was very weak.

The radio operator put his hand over the mouthpiece. "I've got him," he said gaily. He took his hand away. "How ya doin' Chris?"

Electrified by the news that he was still alive, everyone let out a cheer.

Instead of feeling relief, Sky felt more bitterness. *Why'd you have to go down after something you don't even know positively is there, or alive?*

Cuppy's loud voice interrupted her anger. "You better get your ass up here right now. You're already 22 minutes past your down time. Where are you," he yelled.

"Dunno."

"Do you have the child?" It was Dr. Isu.

"Yes."

"Is she okay?" This time it was Phil.

"Yes, I think so," he said, giving an unseen nod. His panting came harder and faster. He wanted to ask Cuppy what had happened to him and the others, but didn't have the time or the strength.

A cheer rippled through the room.

Unaware of acuteness of the situation, Phil cried out, "The world's gonna hear about this. It's a miracle. A miracle I tell ya," He was grinning from ear to ear. Sweat was breaking out in relief. He rushed out to tell the listening and viewing world of the wonderful news. His heart gave an exultant tug, although he didn't allow the excitement that had taken possession of him to show on the surface. He wiped away the tears that laughter brought to his eyes. Quickly he rushed through the door.

The doctor, who was metering his breathing, to his credit, merely lifted an eyebrow as he held up his hand, like and orchestra conductor. "His sand is running out," he whispered. "He's got to come up now."

Everyone fell silent. They were knit together by a common trepidation.

Sky's eyes stung as they suddenly flooded with tears. She knew from the sound of his voice that what the doctor said was true. She lowered her head and touched the bridge of her nose with her thumb and forefinger, as if it would stop the flow of tears. "I knew something was going to go wrong."

Dr. Malik's eyes peered at her over the rim of her glasses. "Have faith my child. He will be alright."

All right, my ass, she thought, *he's not your man.* Sky twisted a rubber band round and round her fingers to keep others from knowing, that to stop, her hands would tremble out of control.

"But he is my friend."

Sky's head snapped up to look her directly in the eye. *Did she read my mind?*

For an awkward moment they silently stared at each other. Dr. Malik's smiled turned to a look of deep compassion and she held her arms out to her. Sky stood frozen to the spot. *If it weren't for you, he wouldn't be down there. You probably encourage him so you could get written up somewhere. Now look what's happening. He'll die and you'll still be here. I hate you for that.*

Dr. Malik's face looked shocked. She straightened her spine, looked once more at Sky, then turned and walked away.

Sky knew she had read her thoughts and now regretted having them. *It's not her fault. It's not anybody's fault. It was destined, regardless of the results. I just want him back alive.*

She looked across the room at Dr. Malik, who had taken a seat against the wall. Telepathically Sky tried to send her a message. *I'm sorry. I didn't mean that. Forgive me.*

As if she heard her, Dr. Malik straightened and smiled in her direction.

Nervous and lacking something to do with her hands, Sky reached for Cuppy. He took both of her hands and held them fast. "Take it easy Sky. He's okay. You can see he's okay," he said unconvincingly. He cradled her in his arms and kissed her on top of the head in an unprecedented display of affection. He then gently pushed her head back with his thumb, "He'll be okay, I promise."

Secretly she was never sure about the dreams so never encouraged Chris to talk about them. How could she persuade him she believed something she wasn't sure of herself? All the while he was down, the sick fear for him crawled around inside her, gnawing away at everything that would keep her alive until he returned. Now she could hear the life running out of him.

Cuppy tried to sound excited enough for both of them, but in his gut he knew Chris was in deep trouble, and it would be getting deeper. His time down had lapsed more than 22 minutes ago and that meant trouble with a capital T. He wondered if he remembered the pony that he had attached to his tanks. He turned and snatched the microphone from the radioman.

"Yeah. I'm a hero," Chris laughed weakly, but there was no humor in it.

"Chris, the pony," his voice firm and clear. "Did you remember the pony?"

There was another prolonged pause.

Time went as slowly as a snail's trip from Chattanooga to a California cabbage patch as they awaited a reply.

Lou felt his stomach knot. He couldn't stand the waiting and wanted to do something…anything. He hated feeling so helpless.

Sky took the mike from Cuppy. She hesitated for a fraction of a second. When she did speak, it was more like a business voice—-to the point and unemotional. "Dr. Healy. You are to stop what you are doing and return to the surface immediately. You have passed your down time. Head for the surface right now. I mean, right now!" That was perhaps an outrageous demand. She did not think so. It was not a hostile command, but a statement of fact she thought.

There was a prolonged silence. Contact was lost. The men exchanged concerned glances.

Cuppy stood next to her. "I don't thin…"

She looked at him in irritation and motioned him to remain silent.

Indignation flickered in his eyes.

They waited. Still there was no response. Their fear for his safety held them as firm as any nightmare.

She turned and buried her head in Cuppy's shoulder. Terror held her immobile.

He held her for a moment, and then gently held her away from him. He placed his hands on either side of her face. "We're not going to give up." He felt her warm tears trickle over his fingers, which embarrassed him as she had never let him see her so vulnerable. "He's going to be okay. We mustn't lose faith. He'll be back aboard before we know it. I'm gonna go down just to make sure. I'll bring him up." *Dead or alive,* he thought. "I promise."

He turned abruptly and shouted, "I want a team down at the site right now. I want the best. Do you hear me, the best? He might need help and we're all standing around like idiots with our thumbs up our ass. Suit up. I'll meet you on deck in two minutes." He turned back to Sky, "I'll take care of him, you can bet your girdle on that." Sky forced a smile but it did not change the fear in her eyes.

He had been diving over 20 years, but in diving, there was always some moment or two when he imagined death itself. Would he run out of air, be trapped in some wreck, or maybe be attacked by a shark? He tried to put it out of mind and focus on the job ahead. *I won't let you down buddy,* he thought, this *is not your time...not if I have anything to do with it.* His deepest sadness for Chris now was that he couldn't be where he was. He glanced over to Dr. Isu, Dr. Malik, Sky and the doctor, and then turned to leave.

"We'll be praying for you," Dr. Malik said softly.

With equal quiet, Sky said, "Bring him back safe."

"Are the cameras recording? What about the television transmission," Phil asked the cameraman. He straightened his posture and addressed the surrounding boats as if he were about to direct the Philharmonic orchestra.

The waiting crowd looked expectant as Phil prepared to give his report. A buzz of murmuring sounded aboard the nearby boats.

Meanwhile, all over the world, big screen TV's were tuned to the same station. In millions of homes people stood transfixed before their sets, in awed silence, waiting for brief updates. Phil continued to report the unfolding drama, which was informative and accurate. All felt helpless. All wanted to help. But all they could do now is watch and wait. The fate of this child touched the world.

Phil's voice was clear, concise and well modulated. "Ladies and gentlemen. We are reporting live from 120 miles off of the island of

Honolulu, Hawaii. On this very spot the luxurious ocean liner *Emperor,* with all hands aboard, was sent 160 feet to the bottom by two freak Tsunamis just hours ago. The only survivor, we believe, is a child, that was thought to be born, after her mother had boarded the ship. The E*mperor* was traveling to Japan when this terrible disaster struck. We have just made contact with Dr. Chris Healy, the diver who risked his life to rescue this child from the bowels of the sunken liner."

"Again, we are here live above the wreck of the *Emperor,* and have just made contact with Dr. Healy. He has found the child alive...alive, ladies and gentlemen, and is working his way through the wreckage while carrying this tiny infant in a specially devised self-sustaining chamber. He will bring the child to the surface in a matter of moments, ladies and gentlemen, so stay tuned to our live joint broadcast from TXXM and the *Honolulu Gazette*." The wrinkles about his eyes smiled as he reported further facts and figures about the *Emperor* and its passengers.

The jubilant crowds, elated with the news, cheered, whistled, and clapped in celebration.

People around the world, setting off a mood of near euphoria, were dancing and cheering, laughing and crying. They set off guns and firecrackers. Masses were running into the streets where they shook hands, hugged and kissed each other. All were sure the child would be rescued.

They were not aware of the dilemma below.

10:54 A.M. June 6

Chris knew he wasn't going to make it. He felt the chill of death breathing on him. He no longer could feel his hands and feet. The cold was claiming the outer layers of his body. He was colder than a sadist's heart. Any moment he expected the constriction of air in his mouthpiece, a sign that his air supply was nearing exhaustion. Suddenly, without warning, he was out of air. The mouthpiece did not constrict as expected.

A kaleidoscope of colors flashed across his eyes. Sweat was blooming on his forehead. His heart was beating heavily on his side. He felt the chill of death breathing on him. In spite of this, there was something more intense, something that went deeper than personal survival that made him want to drive on. He had to save this child…his sister's child. Nothing else mattered.

His vision was beginning to blur even more. *I'm not going to make it.* He lay there for a few moments longer, eyes fixed on the light, lest he lose sight of it. He knew there wasn't much time to bring the child to the surface. He struggled to his feet, panting under the effort and followed the light. When he thought he was finally getting nearer, it would turn a corner…as if it were waiting for him to catch up before it turned. He followed although he didn't know why.

He fell again. Exhausted, and out of air, he started to lose consciousness. He could feel movement around him but his eyes just wouldn't open. Suddenly there was fresh oxygen coming into his facemask. Coughing, he breathed deeply in and out several times. *Where did this come from,* he wondered. Then he remembered the pony Cuppy had attached to his tanks. He looked down to see the J valve had been moved to the open position. *The regulator should have warned me…but how….*

He looked around. No one was there. The light down the corridor waited for him.

Hungry for air, he called on his last reserve of strength. He called out to the unknown, "I'm not gonna make it…." His strength was fading. Sweat ran onto his face. The stars crossing his eyes were colorful. His aching limbs felt as though the sins of the world were secretly attached when he wasn't looking. His throat was parched and he ached for a drink.

In his surrender of his approaching death, he called out, "God, help me!"

Abruptly the phantom of his mind appeared to him. She smiled gently and sadly as she motioned him to move toward the light. "Come my brother. Follow me. You must hurry. Come...come...." Her form moved gracefully down the corridor.

Move toward the light? My God am I dead and just don't know I?.

With great effort he pushed himself, not caring now if she was a hallucination or not, or if he was dead or not. He knew he had to save the child, even if he perished himself. His lungs were barely moving air.

10:59 A.M. June 6

As he moved down the passageway, he became weaker and weaker. Numbness and tingling were spreading quickly through his body.

Fight was fading from his eyes. Unable to continue, he collapsed. His body slowly floated toward the ceiling. Chris knew he was dying when he felt himself slipping from his physical body yet he still clung to the tiny receptacle.

Suddenly there was a sense of rapid movement around him. He felt as though he was entering into a different energy dimension. The motion around him was a distinctive different density than that of the cold water in which he floated. Motionless and helpless, he could see cloud-like visions moving around him. His tortured mind and body felt peaceful and quiet with no pain. It was an exquisite peace that comes when a deep fear is removed. He knew he was dead.

Gently a warm hand was placed on his head. Suddenly his spirit pulled back into his body and the spark of life returned. The energy near him appeared to be electrifying every atom in his body. Through half closed eyes and dreamlike awareness, he saw an indistinct view of these forms moving him through the water. He looked down to see if he still had a hold of the child. Yes, she was still with him. He grasped the handle tighter lest he pass out again and loses his grip.

Through blurry eyes he strained to see who or what it was. He was astonished to see it was a living light, a light far beyond his frail concept of form and substance. It was unlike anything he had ever encountered before.

The energy was not solid, but instead, all around it pure energy emanated; there were no shapes or forms, just free flowing bioluminescence of light. Suddenly the red hair of his sister began to emerge from the light, followed by the rest of her form, which was made up of countless tiny points of interconnected light. She was incredibly beautiful.

"Is that you Patty?"

She smiled softly and nodded.

"I'm dead, aren't I?"

"No, my brother. You will live. It is not your time. You are the guardian of my child."

"But how…"

Without warning her image faded.

He wondered if she wasn't just a manifestation of his own unconscious thoughts.

The darkness swallowed him as he drifted into unconsciousness. He felt exquisite peace where there was no pain. Conversations with Dr. Isu floated through his head. *Undesirable outcome. Fate is not immune to our efforts to change it. These dreams were intended to prepare you men to cope with, not prevent future events.* Pictures flashed across his brain: of the debris field, plates buckling and rupturing, decks collapsing down on each other like an accordion, as they impacted with the bottom, bodies floated by, and then blackness.

Three Dreams

11:04 A.M. June 6

"It has been more than twenty minutes since we lost contact with Chris Healy," Phil reported through trembling lips. "I'm afraid experts are beginning to give up hope of him and the child coming up alive. His surely must have run out by now. Search teams are looking for them at this very moment. As I reported earlier, Mr. Healy's tanks only contained enough air to sustain him for two hours. In our last contact with him he had reached the child and was moving out of the *Emperor*. The child's air could only last seventeen minutes...." Overcome, he moved the mike away. *Oh God, please help them,* he prayed. *I promise I won't drink any more. Please don't let this happen again. I want a second chance, please, please God, give it to me."* He stood silently for a few moments looking up into the sky...perhaps for a sign. None came.

Everywhere around the globe, people huddled around their radios and TVs in order to keep pace with rescue attempts. As the rescue grew more extended Phil's voice became more and graver. Everywhere people were stunned, shocked, and crying with hearing of their possible deaths. A tense waiting hush was upon them. Faces that were smiling before were now agonizing over the fate of Chris and the child. Thousands began to pray.

Sky was doing some praying of her own. Frustrations were piling up and she could feel her nervous tension building like a head of steam. She pressed her hand against her mouth to confine the scream she wanted so desperately to let out. Safeguarding her dignity, she excused herself and retreated to the bathroom. It was tiny compared to what she was used to in her apartment. The miniature vanity basin, soap dispenser, and waste can were all attached to the wall. The mirror above the sink was cracked and cloudy with age.

Sky studied her face in the mirror, for a few moments, then let out a scoffing laugh. Suddenly she broke into heart-wrenching sobs and called out to God. "Please bring him back to me. Please. I love him so much...we're going to have a child together. What will we do without him? What will we do?" He shoulders shook from the deep sobs. Tears streaked her face with mascara.

Sky hadn't told Chris she was expecting. She didn't want to use that as an excuse to marry, nor to trap Chris into proposing. She was planning to tell him on their next romantic date. That would have been the best time, she thought. Now she won't be able to tell him at all. Sobs shook her whole body as she wrapped her arms around her stomach, as if to protect her coming child. "I'm sorry baby, I'm so, so sorry. You'll never get to know what a wonderful man your father was. You see, I was afraid to tell him about you…I was afraid…God I was afraid…."

As she leaned against the sink she got a glimpse of herself in the mirror. She was almost unrecognizable. Her skin was sallow and her red-rimmed eyes were bloodshot. Mascara, mixed with tears, gave her a Raccoon appearance. It had run down her cheeks and onto the front of her blouse. After splashing water on her face she rubbed the mascara out from under her eyes and cheeks, then dabbed at her blouse. When finished she reached for another paper towel. It startled her when it magically appeared in her hand. The overhead light suddenly went on. Startled, she whirled around; thinking someone had entered unnoticed.

For a moment she was too startled to speak. Frightened, she asked, "Who's there?" Her eyes darted about.

To her astonishment a form of a woman stood before her. It wasn't a woman as she had known, but one made up of countless tiny effervescent interconnected lights. She discerned the image had reddish hair. The woman's face was hue less but her eyes shone like green emeralds on a king's crown.

"My God," she gasped. She wondered if it was the same woman Chris had mentioned. A hundred questions assaulted her brain.

Telepathically the form's thought-images answered her questions even before they were asked. A thousand images came swarming to her mind. She 'listened' with absorbed interest as the energy told her of why she was so fearful and reluctant to support Chris in this endeavor.

She felt the pain of the memory of when she was a child and her father was not home very much. Although doted on by her mother, her father rebuked her with angry scorn. Before she was born, he wanted a son, but instead, Sky was born. There were complications with the birth. When he learned his wife could no longer bear children, his mannerisms changed. He kept Sky and her mother in a

Three Dreams

perpetual state of anxiety with his ostentatious, condescending, reserved and distant manner. She felt he merely tolerated her and her mother until finally, one day he left, never to return. When she learned of his death, it caused her little emotion. Now she knew of the conflict in his soul. He blamed himself for the complications, although in reality, it could not have been his fault. She finally understood what her father had gone through and why she was so fearful of Chris undertaking this rescue. She had lost her father suddenly and discovered she had made this transference onto Chris. She was afraid he'd abandon her by not returning. She loved him, just as she had her dad, with such an aching and an all-giving love, that she was afraid he would be taken away. She now realized it was better to love than to stomp on sour grapes.

She told her that, in her search for happiness, she was looking for answers about her father, in Chris. The image communicated that she already knew the answers, and that they laid waiting to de discovered, within her. All she had to do is to look. She showed her, quick as thought, how to move beyond the loss of losing her father and the powerlessness she felt when he went away, and to reach out for the love that was right here, right now. *It's God's port of entry. Step through.*

A calm washed over her. Her fears seemed to drain from her like warm liquid. Even if she could go back, there would be nothing she could do. She realized it was a very personal journey that her father had to travel alone. Now she would travel her own road and not look back.

One of the questions she asked was, if Chris was still alive, but before she received an answer, a knock came at the door.

"You gonna be in there forever," called a voice. "I gotta go…now!"

Distracted, she glanced toward the door. "In a minute," she yelled. When she looked back, the image had vanished.

Startled, and amazed at the intensity of the experience, she staggered from the room and leaned up against the adjacent wall. Quickly, the man in 'need' raced past her, slamming the door behind him. *My God, who was that? Could it be the same one Chris talked about? Where did she come from? Where did she go? Was she an angel or a ghost?*

She felt elated-excited, frightened, and a gamut of other emotions. Taking a few deep breaths Sky, feeling a new balance, raced to see if there was any news of Chris.

11:17 a.m. June 6

Chris could feel his body being guided by the forms to the surface. Again he felt the life ebbing from within. *I can't pass out. I've got to get my niece to the surface before it's too late. I've got to hang on...I've got to....* He lost consciousness again.

Cuppy and three divers were following the down line when they could see Chris's light moving toward them.

"There he is," Pappy yelled.

"By God, he made it. I don't know how, but he made it," says Cuppy, moving faster down the line.

Submerging deeper, Joe says, "That's no lamp down there...wha...what the hell **is** that?"

As they descended they could see a luminescent, almost phosphorescent light below them. It was nothing like any lamp they had seen before. Moving closer they saw several translucent figures surrounding Chris's unconscious body. The five ascending sentinels did not have wings nor halos but the men knew they were not of this world. Each of the figures held one end of a silvery cord-like thread while the other end was attached to Chris's body. Each supported a portion of his body while one supported the chamber.

"Hey, they ain't got no diving gear on," one diver shouted. "Them angels? I thought angels were supposed to float around in heaven or somewhere. Never thought I'd see them here."

As they approached the divers, they silently allowed them to take charge of him and the tiny infant. In a matter of moments they dematerialized, leaving a host of tiny living sapphires, which too melted away in moments.

"Nah, they weren't no angels...they didn't have no wings. Aliens, if ya ask me," refuted another diver. "I wonder what they did to him."

Cuppy shot them a look that spoke a thousand words.

As they turned to head for the surface the red haired sentinel reappeared. She remained suspended for a few moments, as she lovingly looked first to the child and then to Chris. There seemed to be a silent intercommunication between them before she turned to Cuppy.

In telepathic transmission she thanked him for being Chris's friend and for his years of dedication to her brother, for his unwavering belief in him and for assisting in the rescue of her child. She smiled, looked once more to Chris and the child, and then disappeared in a profusion of brilliant emeralds.

The divers looked at each other in disbelief. They couldn't believe their eyes. One of them had run his hand through the emeralds, but they evaporated upon his touch.

Pulling himself together, Cuppy barked, "We didn't see that. We didn't see anything." To him it smacked of Sci-fi hocus-pocus, like the special affects in the movie *The Abyss*. He knew these weren't special affects by any means. Getting a firmer hold on Chris he added, "If anybody says anything, we didn't see nothin'…understand? Nothin'."

Wide eyed, the divers nodded in affirmation and began to transport Chris to the surface while continuously looking over their shoulders all the way to the surface.

They could hear Cuppy murmuring to himself. 'I ain't never seen anything in my life like that. Never. My God, fairies down here. Hum! We tell them that topside, they'll think we're touched.'

Secretly, within he knew exactly who the apparition was. *I knew it, I always knew it,* he thought, and smiled broadly away from the view of the men. *Man, can I call 'em or what?*

Deeply concerned for the child, Pappy attempted to relieve Chris of the chamber, but his intractable fingers would not budge. He knew time had already run out for both of them. The infant appeared lifeless within the chamber.

"I think we've got trouble," Pappy barked. "I don't see any signs of life and he won't let go unless I break his fingers."

Momentarily Cuppy had forgotten about the child. When he riveted his eyes on her, clearly there were no signs of life. "Let's get them to the top **now**," he barked, "we have no time to waste."

11:26 A.M. June 6

Quickly they broke the surface. Cheers, jubilation whoops and whoop hollering emanated from the surrounding boats. Unaware of the seriousness of the situation, they got two thumbs up from their audience.

Cuppy searched for Sky at the rail. Their eyes met. Flipping his facemask off he yelled triumphantly, "I told you I'd bring him back." Secretly he completed the sentence, *dead or alive.*

Tears streaked her cheeks. "Thank you. I'll never forget you for this." She yelled back. This day she thought Cuppy the most wonderful man on earth.

Seconds later Chris was being pulled aboard the *Blue Pelican.* The men laid him gently on the deck and elevated. The doctor knelt beside him, unzipped his wet suit and gave him a cursory examination. He listened to his racing heart, examined his open wounds, peered into his eyes, took his pulse and thumped him here and there while others attempted to remove his grip on the chamber. He could hear men's voices and felt rough hands pulling him from the water, experienced hands that worked quickly and knowingly. A myriad of faces came and went. Hands freed him of his weights, mask, tanks and flippers. Voices were speaking without meaning. He could not get his eyes to focus. He felt hands trying to pry his death grip from the chamber but still he wouldn't let go.

Sky raced to his side.

Everyone circled around, quietly waiting.

"He's alive...just barely...but he is alive. From the looks of his eyes, I suspect he has a concussion. Help me get him to the recompression chamber. Hold on to him, he's starting to convulse." Quickly they crossed the deck to the recompression chamber. "Turn his head to the side, he's choking. Get him in there quickly. Sky, you go in too," ordered Dr Henry. "My assistant can take over from here. Loosen that chamber and let's take her below. Time is crucial."

All the while Cuppy was attempting to remove the chamber from his grip. "It's okay ole buddy, you can let go now. We'll take good care of her, but now the doctor has to check her out," says Cuppy softly but firmly.

For a moment or two Chis's brain refused to work. He would not release the chamber. Suddenly his eyes snapped open.

"You've got to let go and let the doc have a look at her."

Finally he relented. "Her name is Rose," he whispered hoarsely as he loosened his grip in a convulsion. "Rose. Her name is Rose."

"Okay Rose, you come with me. The doc is waiting to check you out." Cuppy reached down and ruffled Chris's hair. "You're going to be okay ole buddy. He gently picked up the tiny box, flashed Chris a smile, and then handed the tiny case to Lou. Without delay both men headed below with their precious cargo.

Sky let out her breath in relief and let her shoulders slump. "He's safe. He's safe. Oh thank you God." Then she started laughing, a joyous bubbly sound from deep in her throat. She dropped to her knees beside him and bent over him, curling her one arm around his head and kissed his face all over.

With her face pressed against his she murmured, "I thought you were dead. I thought I had lost you." Overwhelmed, she then began to cry great gulping sobs.

As he again passed out, he could hear Scott's voice, "A job well done. Hang in there buddy." Bile washed up into his throat.

11:33 A.M. June 6

Quickly Lou ran inside, placed the child gently on the table, and then carefully opened the compression chamber. There laid a tiny baby girl who could not have been more than one to two days old. The dried unbiblical cord was still attached. Her eyes were closed, her lips blue against her ashen face. She didn't appear to be breathing. Clutched in her tiny hand was the cellophane containing the rose.

Phil, half-laughing, half-crying, tried to get a closer look at the infant. Dr. Henry quickly removed the blanket to examine the child. Phil's heart skipped a beat when saw the birthmark on her leg. To his amazement, he saw it was very much like the one his daughter was born with. He thought his heart would leap out of his chest.

Doctor Henry hastily examined the infant for signs of life. Everyone waited. After a few moment of listening through his stethoscope he somberly he shook his head. "I'm sorry. She's gone."

She's dead. How can that be? Why did you bring her back to me and then take her away again? How could you have pulled such a dirty trick on me God," Phil thought as he stared at the lifeless form.

People began to cry. Someone ran outside and could be heard calling out the sad news to the other boats. All cheering suddenly ceased.

Doctors' Isu and Malik stood like two statues staring at the child. A slight smile could be detected on the edge of Dr. Isu's lips. No one noticed.

D.C.'s eyes glistened. He coughed to clear the boulder from his throat, and then fled to the men's room where he sobbed deeply into a towel.

"I don't care," he repeated over and over, "I don't care. Oh God, why did you let this happen," he called out, shaking his fist in the air. Since he had witnessed five friends drown when his ship went down in a storm; he had shut down his feelings. He fought to keep his buddies alive, but in the end, he was the lone survivor. Since that time he suffered survivor's guilt. This rescue was the first time he really felt any deep emotion since then. He sobbed hard and deep, not only for the infant but also perhaps for his lost comrades as well.

Phil glanced about uncertainly, as if he was hoping someone would tell him it was a terrible mistake. Pushing the doctor aside, his arms reached down for the lifeless child and pulled her tightly to him as if trying to pull her to the center of his grief. Tears ran down his face and dropped onto her lifeless cheek. She was very cold. Phil pulled open his jacket and gently wrapped her limp body inside. "Rose. Rose. It's daddy," he cried into her cheek. His pleading eyes looked from face to face, hoping someone could revive her. "It's daddy. Can you wake up for daddy?" The child did not hear him.

Mouths dropped open; everyone stared, in disbelief, at the tiny lifeless face just visible above Phil's lapel. The silence aboard the boat spread like an early morning fog. Someone behind him sobbed without tears. A dry, breathless sound, a nothing-to-hope-for cry. Soft sobs escaped some onlookers while silent tears ran down their faces. Others dissolved in tears and ran from the room.

Chris slowly returned to sensibility on a slow motion wave of prismatic lights. He hadn't felt the anti-tetanus injection he received as he squinted to focus toward the portals at the silent people on deck. The tiniest of moves caused him pain. Through glazed eyes he saw the people who were excited moments ago, were now gathered around soundless. Many were crying. He heard words, but could not yet comprehend their meaning.

Before he blacked out he asked, "The child?"

The assistant stood straight up and let out a long low sigh. Although six-foot-one, he seemed to grow inches in the anger he felt. He fought to keep his voice low. "I'm afraid the baby didn't make it."

Chris went unconscious.

Phil's laughed a desperate laugh, which was perilously close to a scream. He then began to sob. His cries broke everyone's hearts. Everyone huddled together instinctively, keeping their eyes, with a sort of horrified fascination, on the child. Doctors' Isu and Malik, Lou, Sky and Cuppy gathered around him. Everyone circled around staring at the sight, which confronted him or her. Then one person placed their arm around another, then another, and soon Phil was circled by their love. The room was still, save the pleadings coming from Phil, trying to will the child back to life.

Oh baby, come back to daddy. I'm here. Come back to daddy. I've waiting so long for you. Oh Rose…baby…please come back to daddy. **Oh God**," he shouted, **"please help my baby."** He pulled her

Three Dreams

closer to him and wept sorrowfully, like a man would, with a broken heart.

All of a sudden the heavy air was surcharged with a brilliant light. Its luminescence was almost a spiritual-like glow, the likes that none had seen before. Every one looked up to see what it was. It shone in the room like a private sun so bright; they had to shield their eyes. Slowly it faded to a blue glow, lingered for a few moments, and then it was gone.

Eyes searched the room for evidence of it having been there.

A moment later, "Whaaagh, Whaaagh."

Phil suddenly felt the baby squirming in his arms. He opened his jacket and looked at her in disbelief. He was ecstatic, laughing and crying at the same time, as was everyone else.

"Rose, oh Rose, you came back. Oh Rose, daddy is here baby, daddy is here. Oh thank you God, thank you, thank you." He hugged and kissed her. He held her up for everyone to see.

People patted him on the back.

"Congratulations Phil...."

"It's a miracle man, a miracle."

"I'm so happy for you Phil."

"God bless Phil."

People began laughing and cheering and ran outside to tell the others. Happy voices were screaming to the nearby boats that the child was alive. Boat horns were tooting, people were cheering, whistling, and hugging each other, while others were clasped their hands in prayer, thanking God for the miracle. Eyes brimmed with tears of joy. Some stood silent, awe struck, by the miracle that just befell them.

A voice called out, "I knew you could do it God. I just knew it. You're the Man.!"

Cheers rose up in agreement.

Through the media, word spread throughout the world, of this miracle child's rescue. There was pandemonium. There was applause. There were tears and cries of excitement. People were dancing in the streets while others were down on their knees thanking God for answering their prayers.

Lives would change as a result of this tiny infant. Some disbelievers were now believers. Those who said, "I don't believe a word of it" were now saying, "I knew they could do it, all along."

A wondrous thing had come unto the world.

Chris awoke briefly a little later to find Sky's face just above his own. In his peripheral he could see Dr Henry preparing a syringe. He assumed for him. He was in severe pain and wondered if there was a nitrogen bubble still lodged in his knee joint. Knowing these bubbles could be fatal, or could cause permanent damage to his body if it traveled to his brain, he lay very still.

"The baby...I couldn't...."

She smiled and touched her finger to her lips, silencing him. "Shhh. She's alive and healthy. You saved her. She's a miracle baby. A wonderful, pink, miracle baby because of you."

"Thank God," Chris whispered hoarsely, "and thank you Pat."

Understanding, Sky smiled, and then began to hum softly as she stroked his face softly, until he slept again.

Three Dreams

6:11 p.m. June 7

On shore there was a tumultuous welcome. Police cars, ambulances, emergency vehicles, a sea of reporters, and broadcast trucks we scattered about. Photographers were hanging out of helicopter doors so they could capture the widest-angle possible of the scene. It was chaos.

The sprawling crowd's buzzing excitement broke into a roar when Chris and his team stepped off the boat. Screams and whistles emanated from everywhere. Handkerchiefs and banners waved in the air. Strong powerful lights were trained their way, making it difficult to see where they were going

Scott found Marlene in the crowd and ran to her. "I love you, I love you, I love you. Do you know that? I love you," he said as he scooped her up and twirled her around in the air.

All Marlene could do was cry. It was the day she had waited so long for.

An ambulance was standing by to take Rose to the hospital but Phil wouldn't let the medics take her, insisting he'd hold her all the way. He swore to himself that he'd never let go of 'his' little girl again. "Isn't that right honey? We'll take care of her all the way," he says to his wife, as he pressed closer to her.

She smiled, thanking God under her breath for the transformation this child brought to his life. "Yes darling, that's right…we'll take care of her…forever."

As Chris and Sky strolled down the pier she asked, "Do you think Phil will have any trouble adopting her?"

"I don't expect so. She's my niece and I can't think of a better set of parents for her." Earlier Chris had verbalized to Scott of his concern for Phil's obsession with the child. Scott then related the circumstances in the crib death of Phil's daughter. Gaining an understanding, he knew he would not stand in the way when Phil wanted to adopt her, even though, legally, he had first rights. "Thinks she the reincarnation of his daughter…but who's to say it isn't?"

"Do you understand any of this," Sky asked as she placed her arm his waist.

"No, not really." Pause. "Think we should have one of those," he asks, jutting his jaw in the direction of the baby.

"Would you want a boy or a girl," she asked.

"A girl would be nice, but then again, so would a boy."

" We have six months to find out which it is."

He stopped dead in his tracks and stared into her eyes. "Really?"

"Yes, Really." She was not afraid.

His eyes became blinded with tears. He could not think why.

Lives changed after that, and for the better. D.C. had originally received his nickname because he was always saying, I **Don't Care**, now insists on it reading I **Do Care**. Lou, who invented the apparatus that saved the child, decided he would focus his inventions on helping save the lives of other children, and left the sea. Scott and Marlene sold their house and moved close to the beach. He has stopped drinking and is a proud father of twin boys. He still accurately predicts earthquakes to this day. Lucky? Well, Lucky just felt ever so lucky to be a part of this wondrous miracle. Talks about it all of the time. Cuppy still worries over the baby and won't let anyone get too close, lest she catch germs…after all; he's an Uncle now. Phil is acting like a proud parent with all the fussing he does over her. Dr. Malik was the baby's physician until she reached land. She was glad to report that Rose suffered no ill after affects. She now continues her research in the paranormal off the coast of Switzerland. Dr. Isu? Dr. Isu disappeared at the dock the day they landed…never to be seen again. One wonders if he decided to retire to his garden, if, indeed, he was ever there. Perhaps he was sent to encourage others into fulfilling their destinies. Perhaps he was an angel. We may never know.

Three Dreams

The journey beyond the brink of death had forever changed Chris' life. This wasn't the end of his dream, but the beginning of a new one. To this day he continues to carry the medal of St. Elmo in his pocket. His sister never again visited him.

Some things have to be believed to be seen.

Ralph Hodgson

Roberta M. Alleman

About the Author

Roberta Alleman, Ph.D., is a counselor in Human Behavior, educator and author. She was born in Boston, MA but was moved to San Diego, CA as a young child. After High School she married and had four children. She became involved in Vietnam Vet issues and is responsible for April 22nd being designated as a National Day of Recognition for Vietnam vets. She has received commendations from the President, all the way to the local Mayor, for her dedication to these vets and their families.